The Woollen Olive Branch

A North and South Festive Retelling

Caroline Malcolm-Boulton

Copyright

Author: Caroline Malcolm-Boulton.
Published and printed by Amazon.
First Printed: 2022.
Current number of editions: 1.
This edition: 1.
ISBN: 9798370580765.

This book contains quotes from Elizabeth Gaskell's *North and South*. This text is now in the public domain, so copyright restrictions are no longer applicable.
This book contains references to the BBC Adaptation of *North and South* (2004). Permission has been granted for this book to be published by the relevant BBC department, along with the screenwriter for the series, Sandy Welch.

Cover Illustration: Canva.

Dedication

This book is dedicated to Elizabeth Gaskell, without whose creative intelligence and integrity, this work would not have been made possible. I cannot begin to imagine what Gaskell would have thought of fan fiction, or what she would have thought of this humble Christmas tale that draws inspiration from her literary creation. But I hope and trust that it would have made her smile to see her beloved characters, her John and Margaret, share in their love, and that 168 years after her empowering and endearing novel was written, people still care about their story.

I would also like to dedicate this book to my daughter, Arabella. Bella is my husband, Scott, and I's first child, born in April 2022. Writing has always been a passion of mine, and while I am delighted to be a mother, I am not abashed to admit that I was concerned that motherhood would prevent me from attaining my own personal and creative aspirations. Therefore, this book, my own first published work, is dedicated to my daughter, because I want to show her that women can be good and dedicated mothers, whilst also realising their own dreams. So here's to 2022, and my two cherished babies!

Introduction

The Woollen Olive Branch is a festive retelling of Elizabeth Gaskell's *North and South*, which was originally published in 1854. This section is for those who are acquainted with the novel and would like an understanding of at which point in the narrative this story begins, or likewise, for those who are not familiar with Gaskell's work, and would therefore like to apprise themselves of the context.

North and South is an English classic which compares and contrasts elements of Victorian society, highlighting the discord that often existed (and sadly still does to an extent), between seemingly opposing factions, such as: the north and south of England, rich and poor, life and death, masters and workers, faith and atheism, men and women, and the past and present. Gaskell's enlightening novel seeks to challenge these distinctions through showing us that people should be judged not by their class, but by their character, and that we can seek to heal the divisions in society if we are willing to recognise and appreciate the individual's right to self-determination.

The novel begins in London, where the eighteen-year-old Margaret Hale is to leave her aunt and cousin after years of living with them and return to take up permanent residence with her mother and father in the idyllic country hamlet of Helstone in southern England. However, not long after Margaret returns to her childhood home, her father announces his intention to relinquish his vocation as a clergyman, and relocate his family to the northern, industrial town of Milton. The Hales then find themselves thrust into the energetic and unequal world of a manufacturing metropolis, where masters and their money hold the power, one of whom becomes her father's pupil, John Thornton.

Thornton is a man in his late twenties, and is highly regarded amongst his peers as an exceedingly successful and shrewd cotton merchant, as well as a venerated magistrate. He is a man who has known strife, having lost his father several years before, plunging his family into poverty. As a result, Thornton is a man who is no stranger to the trials of life, his experiences have taught him self-denial, and leaving him with an innate insecurity about his position as a gentleman in an ever-changing socio-economic world.

While there is an evident attraction between Margaret and Thornton, their divergent backgrounds lead them to frequently spar as they struggle to understand each other's principles and points of view. However, despite their tempestuous acquaintance, Thornton cannot help but fall in love with Margaret, a woman whom he admires for her integrity of mind and independence of spirit. Therefore, after a turbulent event which forces them to consider their feelings for one another, Thornton proposes, but Margaret refuses, leaving him hurt and humiliated by her rejection, and she is awakened by the first embers of love.

In the following weeks, Margaret's brother, Frederick, who is living in exile abroad because of trouble with the navy, returns to England in secret to see his dying mother one last time, with nobody in Milton knowing that he exists, including Thornton. Later, when she is furtively saying farewell to her brother at Outwood train station, Margaret is seen with him by Thornton, the mill master observing her embracing a young man in the dark.

In light of this, along with the lies she later tells to hide the fact that she was there at all that night, Thornton's jealousy grows as he questions her integrity and her relationship to the handsome stranger, leading him to verbally lash out at her one night, and openly challenge her trustworthiness.

It is at this point that *The Woollen Olive Branch* commences. While Gaskell's original novel, and the 2004 series, provide two different and very beautiful conclusions to this classic tale, my retelling revises the end of *North and South*, exploring an alternative way for our lovers to confess their shared feelings for one another, and come together in love.

Before We Were Us

Caroline Malcolm-Boulton, also known as The Scribbler CMB, has written *North and South* retellings and continuations under the following patented titles:

Before We Were Us
The Thornton Tales
A Marriage of Inconvenience
Parodies and Other Such Poppycock
Criss-Cross-Crossovers

This book belongs to the series *Before We Were Us.*

Before We Were Us is a series which explores a variety of narrative possibilities to bring *North and South's* Margaret Hale and John Thornton together in different ways, some of which draw inspiration from the novel, others from the 2004 screen adaptation, and some taking on an original premise.

Contents

John turned it over in his hands to inspect it more closely. It was perfect in its imperfection. It was lengthy and thick, but not extravagant in either way, and the yarn was robust yet delicate, promising to wrap his neck in woollen warmth. There were tiny holes here and there marked by frogging, nothing really, but it was charming to think, rendering it seamless to his eye, because it told him that Margaret, despite her flawlessness, could make mistakes. The thought that she had made this with evident care caused his heart to gallop in his chest, and while his former self would have doubted that true forethought had been knitted into its folds, loop by loop, there was a demonstration of dedication to every purl. But there was one detail which interested him the most.

The Woollen Olive Branch

Chapter One

And Then He Was Gone

Breathing heavily in a state of anxious anticipation, Margaret Hale was careful to ensure that her fingertip alone, the most miniscule of measurements, was sanctioned to pull back the edge of her lace curtain as she peered out onto the street below.

Her chest was tight.

Her stomach was churning.

Her head was light.

Her skin was burning.

She felt ill.

She felt alive!

Margaret could sense it, that oh-so familiar feeling that only ever happened when –

What was that?

A voice?

No, she thought not.

A shuffle?

Perhaps.

A cough?

Most likely.

Oh! Why was it so hard to tell?

She shook her head, for it was her own fault, of course it was.

Margaret would be much better placed to learn all she wanted to know if only she would go –

There!

There it was again.

It was unquestionably a sound of some description, one that had interrupted the silence which had previously deafened her ears. It was a positively conspicuous noise, yet at the same time, it was a hopelessly indistinctive one, something she could make neither head nor tail of. With her body stiffening, Margaret made sure that she stood as still as a statue, not a bone, nor a muscle, nor a nerve being permitted to so much as twitch. Here she waited. She...

No! This would not do. This would not do at all.

Twirling round on her left foot, because every detail is imperative at a time like this, lest one put a foot wrong and spoil everything, Margaret came to face the door of her bedroom, a door that was firmly closed, she had made sure of it. Sucking her bottom lip, she thought carefully, very carefully, and then, finally, after the briefest of moments spent in nervous calculation, Margaret took a deep breath and nodded unconquerably.

Yes!

She *would* go. There was no other way around it.

Striding across the room as if it were the most ordinary thing to do, even if it were the most ordinary thing to do in normal circumstances, of which this was anything but, Margaret snatched the handle of her door and flung it open purposefully, all before she sneaked out into the corridor, her every intrepid move just that little bit more hesitant, even if they were somehow more hopeful by contrast. Creeping towards the landing, Margaret was wary of the floorboards that creaked, threatening to give her position away with their betraying Judas squeaks. Reaching out, she took hold of the railing, and there she leaned over, her hands coming to rest on the ledge, her knuckles turning white as she unconsciously gripped it for dear life. With ears as astute as a rabbit's, she listened, every groan the house proffered a clue that Margaret's senses soaked up and analysed, and at last, her recklessness, her bravery, if you will, they were rewarded.

'Thank you for coming,' came a voice, one she knew extremely well, but it was not the one she was eager to hear, prompting her nails to tap impatiently on the lacquered wood of the handrail and score tiny marks of irritation in the russet varnish.

No reply…

Come now! They had to be talking to somebody – *anybody*! Although, not just anyone would do, it had to be a certain someone to satisfy Margaret's curiosity. But still, there surely must be a second person, because it was inconceivable that one would be thanking oneself for attending one's own house. That would be quite mad!

Still nothing…

Ah-ha! There it was. She was sure of it.

Tilting a little further over the ledge, Margaret crooked her head so that she could catch more of the conversation, even if the angle was terribly uncomfortable, the rung digging into her ribs and causing a welt to take up residence, evidence of her absurdity that she would need to either conceal from or explain to Dixon next time the maid helped her dress. Margaret was not accustomed to being nosy, so all of this prying felt most unnatural to her. She valued her own privacy, and therefore, she likewise respected other people's, as she always had. Still, there were some occasions that cried out for a little audacity, and this was most definitely one of them.

So why would they not speak up?

They were doing it on purpose. To vex her, to annoy her, to…to hurt her.
Margaret felt her heart spasm in her chest in retaliation to such a cruel thought.
But no, they would never be so unkind, since callousness was not in their nature, for it did not correspond with the honour of their character.

That is, he would not…*would he*?

Surely he did not know she was here. Or, that is to say, he probably knew she was here, but not that she was *here*. As in, he would know that Margaret was in the house, that much was permissible, this fact could not avoid being divulged. However, what he did not know, and more critically, what he could not be allowed to find out, was that she was closer than he thought, on the very next floor. Only, this time, she was standing right above –

'Oh!'

Margaret gasped and clapped a smothering hand over her mouth as she hurled herself backwards. Tripping over her hem, which became bunched hazardously beneath her feet as she faltered, she stumbled, albeit quietly, and then she curled up into a ball and huddled, hiding as she knelt beside the skirting boards, her clothes promptly becoming covered in dust.

Had he...had he seen her?

Margaret could feel her palms sweating as she refused to let her hand slip from her mouth for fear of making so much as a peep. As vigilantly as she could, she slanted her body closer to the railing, giving her eyes leave to peer below.

Nothing. Nobody.

But she was sure she had just seen...she could have sworn that...

Ah! There it was again. She had been right.

A shock of thick, black hair came into view once more in the hallway below. That is, the hair was not alone, not unaccompanied, of course not, for such a thing would be ludicrous, because hair does not just wander about by itself.
Oh! Margaret could have scolded herself for even entertaining such a silly thought. She was a grown

woman, a sensible person, so why was she behaving like such an inexcusable fool? However, Margaret did not have time to think about this, because at that precise moment, the hair moved again, and this time, a face appeared in its place, glancing upwards, looking towards her, directly at her. She backed away for a second time, the spindles of the banister casting vertical shadows across her like black, branded tarnishes, and Margaret could not help but feel they were mocking her, implying that by hiding away here, by confining herself so, she was creating a prison for her sorry self to languish in, an irony that was all too true.

'Is something the matter?' the first voice asked, the only voice, really, since that was the only one she had heard thus far, even if she knew that another did indeed exist.

'Aye,' came a reply, and that single sound alone felt like the provoking exuding of melted chocolate dripping inside her, the warmth so delicious as it seeped into her every crevasse, sticking to her bones, sliding down her nerves.

'I thought…,' but then the second voice, the far more thrilling voice faltered, unsure of itself.

What came next, was an excruciating hush, and Margaret dreaded that her heartbeat, so loud and intense, could be heard booming throughout the house. Even if Margaret could see nothing, she could feel everything, a pair of penetrating eyes boring through the structure of the Crampton dwelling as they searched, combing every inch of timber and brick, scrutinising the very spot upon which she knelt.

'*Never mind*,' was the final verdict, one that was delivered sharply, and more than a mite gruffly, and from what Margaret could tell, the head had moved once again, the face no longer looking upwards towards her, but instead, it was forward facing, towards the door, no doubt towards an uncharted future, a future she had been told she had no hope of featuring in.

But there was no time to think about that now, not when the two voices were back at it, talking once again. Only now, they were drifting, they were straying away from her, further and further away, and so, she was forced to stand up, and this time, Margaret's daring was even more dauntless, causing her to tiptoe along the passageway and take a few stealthy steps down the stairs. There she sat, her knees tucked beneath her as she crouched like a cat in wait, and there she would stay, for now, anyway. It felt like an age of nothingness, only a few wispy words floating into her ears every now and again, their accuracy difficult to discern and all too easy to discredit.

'I cannot find them anywhere. Have you by any chance seen them?'

'No, I am sorry, I have not, but I will let you know if I do. In the meantime, can I not lend you something? You must concede, or else, my dear man, you will surely freeze.'

A lightsome laugh was conjured, one she had rarely heard before, and not for some time.

'Do not worry, I am hardier than I look.'

Then it all died away, their exchange infuriatingly indiscernible. But then, all of a sudden, Margaret perceived the patent sound of the front door closing, and as quick as the snap of a finger and thumb, she was up and off. Dashing back towards her bedroom, Margaret made her way to the window, and there, throwing caution to the wind, she tore back the curtain in full, the sunlight blinding her for a moment, leaving her quite dizzy and disorientated. Finally, once her vision restored to its full clarity, Margaret found herself staring out at the busy metropolis which still went on out there, without so much as a passing care for what happened within that obscure house, which stood at the end of an obscure street, putting up, and putting up with, a family that Milton judged to be obscure with all their supposedly fine and foreign ways. It was strange because she knew that nothing had changed, not really, not in the grand scheme of things, but as far as Margaret was concerned, nothing would ever be the same again, that is, not unless her whole world was returned to order and set right, and only one person could do that, but whether they would, was an entirely separate matter. Feeling a seed of sadness scatter and sew in the recesses of her heart, Margaret sniffed. It was true, everything had ceased to matter the very moment he had –

Margaret leapt back, the net cloth falling back into place as she relinquished her quivering hold, and she held a hand to her belly, the butterflies within fluttering so frantically, that she could scarcely draw breath, their tiny wings leaving her feeling faint with their incessant flapping, a disconcerting sensation for a woman who was typically unflappable. Despite having withdrawn, Margaret could still see through the thin veil of her curtain, the delicate material like a shrouded screen that gave her a concealed view, whilst at the same time denying anybody on the other side the same furtive right.

Yes, there he was.

He was standing there, just standing there, on the steps, looking up towards her, snow falling all around in a cluster of a thousand snowflakes. He could not observe her, for Margaret knew that nobody could see in, because she had tried and failed before to see into her own bedroom from the street when the curtain was drawn. Nonetheless, there he stood all the same, for quite some time, his eyes fixed, his expression blank, and yet the steady rising and falling of his masculine chest was enough to tell her of the unrest he felt, that chaotic turmoil that lives not on the surface, and is never shown on one's face, but is confined to writhe and war within.

Well, at least she could still make him feel something.

He had sighed, his shoulders wilting, and after putting on his hat, the man strode off along the street and out of sight, never once glancing back, even if her gaze never once deserted him, forever remaining loyal to his retreating shadow.

And then, just like that, he was gone.

Chapter Two

Hearts are Funny Things

It was as Margaret stood by the window, her heart full of an incomprehensible combination of regret and relief, that she detected the thud of familiar footsteps coming up the stairs, their steady plod a sound she had known since childhood. Scurrying away from her lookout post, Margaret snatched up an arbitrary bundle of sewing and went to sit in a chair at the far end of the room, her head bent low as if in deep concentration. Her door then groaned as it opened, its hinges parched and in need of oil, the sound akin to a weary old butler announcing with strained exertion that she had a visitor. A few seconds later, a head appeared around the frame. This same head had tuffs of thinning hair, the strands peppered with white and grey. A little further down was a wrinkled face on which the most noticeable display was a set of thin-wired spectacles perched upon a nose, circles of glass which enlarged a set of soft, blue eyes. At first, the visitor's absent-minded regard trailed around the room, but then, when they eventually saw her, a broad smile graced that familiar face.

'There you are, poppet,' came a gentle voice, as wistful as a whistle on the wind, with just a hint of wisdom to be found there too.

'Good evening, Father,' Margaret replied, her eyes still trained on her needle, the sharp stem of silver flying deftly back and forth through the thin fabric of her handkerchief, her stitches untidy and uneven, her trembling fingers unable to calm themselves.

The smile that had been on Mr Hale's face spread, so much so that it reached the creases of his cheeks and settled within, profound lines which spoke of a man who had lived many a year, tell-tale signs of age, much like the rings in the bark of a tree. Margaret was grateful to see him beam so, since to her mind, her father smiled all too rarely these days. It was true, Mr Hale was downcast in spirit, his heart incapable of joining in with the joy of the season, but despite this melancholy, he was thankful that while he had been forced to say goodbye to his son and wife this year, albeit in different ways and for different reasons, he still had his Margaret, and he prayed daily that she would never be taken from him.

Licking his dry lips, he casually announced: 'We were just talking about you.'

Margaret stilled at once.

An inadequate '*Oh?,*' was all that Margaret could manage to pronounce, a prickly flush sprouting on her breast and extending along her arms and neck like a wildfire.

Mr Hale nodded his head sagely as he went to stand by the window, a mutual focal point, it would seem, his hands clasped behind his back as he tapped his shoes together, a peculiar habit his own father had done when addressing his children on matters that made him uncomfortable.

'Yes, yes we were. Mr Thornton noticed your absence...*again.*'

Margaret shuffled awkwardly in her seat. 'And what did you say?' she asked, trying her best to sound utterly disinterested, her eyes peering up with shy intent to heed what he had to say.

Even though she could not see it, her father creased his brow in confusion, because what people did not know, was that while the Oxford scholar was vastly intelligent, he was also a terribly simple man with a terribly simple way of thinking, and consequently, he could never quite fathom anything vaguely complicated when it came to human interactions.

'Why, the truth,' he said plainly. 'What else would I tell him? It is Mr Thornton, after all. We need never hide anything from John.'

The daughter's head ducked down once more, the very same blush now leaving her face as red as a strawberry. She wanted to tell her father that he was wrong, that sometimes one did have a need to hide things from Mr Thornton, but not out of deception, no, but out of an unselfish desire to protect him, to do right by him. To be sure, because while some would assume that a man of such staunch principle as Mr Thornton, what with all his natural discernment and acumen, would require no safeguarding whatsoever, they would be most wrong indeed, for it is the noblest of men that compel this defence, for if he were to be sullied by a crisis of conscience, especially on her behalf, then it would be shameful to them both.

'Besides, he is so exceptionally clever, that I doubt anybody could ever hide anything from him,' Mr Hale went on, proud of his favourite pupil and his sharp wits, the likes of which he had never met a match for. In consequence, Mr Hale often felt sorry for Mr Thornton. The young man was remarkably well-informed, his mind fertile and inquisitive, invariably relentless in his hunger for knowledge on every theme. Yet, despite his inherent aptitude, for reasons that were not his fault, he had been unable to attain the education he deserved and sorely wanted, and so, Mr Hale, this man of Christian charity, felt it his privileged duty to do whatever he could to help him achieve his academic aspirations, even if this meant just sitting and talking with Mr Thornton by the fireside once a week.

'No, I suppose you are right,' Margaret agreed, thinking on how Mr Thornton had that uncanny ability to work everything and everybody out, no detail being too insignificant to escape his shrewd attention. Margaret judged that, out of all the people in the world, she should know this of him better than most. He could do that to her, work her out, almost like he could see right through her, a skill that was both disconcerting and reassuring all at once.

'At any rate, I told him that you were not well today. I mentioned that you had complained of a headache, and that you were not yourself,' Mr Hale continued, thinking how unfortunate it was that Margaret's ailment had only just come on a mere hour before Mr Thornton's arrival.

She paused. 'And he did not mind?' Margaret checked, guilt gnawing away at her. Her father was entirely correct, she had not been herself of late, but if truth be told, she had been perfectly well, certainly well enough to receive company, but alas, she just could not bring herself to be in the same room as him, not since…not since….

'On the contrary, he minded very much,' Mr Hale asserted adamantly. 'He seemed most anxious to fetch a doctor for you, you know how attentive he is, and he is not one to sit idly by when he can be of service. I believe he stood up more than once, determined to go, but I said there was no need, and he eventually sat back down, but he never quite settled. He had a number of questions about your health, such as why you had been ill for so many weeks, suggesting that you might be sickening for something. He was impatient to help in whatever way he could. He asked if you required someone to nurse you, I said no. He asked if you needed tonics prepared, I said no. He asked if you would benefit from time away from Milton in the countryside or by the sea, but I said no. In short, I said that you were well enough, just a little tired. He then insisted that his mother would send one of their maids or cooks to assist you so that you were not so overtaxed, and I said there was no need, but thank you.'

Margaret unconsciously dropped her head to the side and rubbed her chin against her shoulder with coy reserve. How thoughtful he was. She could not imagine anybody else of her acquaintance taking so much trouble over her welfare, and this thought made her feel dreadfully contrite for causing Mr Thornton so much unease. Of course, it went without saying that he was not anxious for her sake, no, not when he had made it clear that she meant nothing to him. All of Mr Thornton's disquiet would undoubtedly be for her father's sake, she knew that, of course she did, but all the same, the idea that he was thinking of her tenderly at all was enough to give birth to a fragile bud of hope in Margaret's heart.

'To be sure, John noticed your absence as soon as he arrived,' her father wittered on, repeating himself. 'He remarked that Dixon let him in again this week. That she took his hat. And then he mentioned it once more when you were not there to serve us tea.'

Margaret scowled at this. 'I am not a servant!' she snapped.

Mr Hale chuckled good-naturedly. 'No, indeed not, my dear. But I must say that Mr Thornton did look sorry when I said you would not be joining us for his lesson.'

'I cannot think why,' she grumbled, still annoyed by the thought that Mr Thornton was expecting her to serve his tea like a maid, but then again, she may have imagined it, but Margaret was sure she had spied him smile to himself once or twice when she poured his cup and handed it over. Actually, now she came to think of it, he had smiled *every time* she had done this, his attention filched the moment she began the preparations, his body leaning forward expectantly, his eyes transfixed on her hands, his own larger ones extended out in mute entreaty as she approached, that long pinkie stretching out to skim her skin, supposedly by accident.

'It is not as if I add anything by being there,' Margaret added hotly, her fingers tingling at the recollection of his touch, something which now felt like a distant memory that faded further and further away with every passing day that they were separated and estranged by their quarrels.

'I am sure that Mr Thornton would hardly notice if I were there or not,' she said miserably, thinking on how she thought of him constantly, always wondering what he was doing, what he was thinking, whether his thoughts ever wandered to her, whether it be aimlessly, or with irrepressible intent.

'That is not true,' her father countered, intrigued by a cart of vegetables that trundled along the street, a rickety wheel making it wobble precariously from side to side, spilling the contents onto the muddy road, the vendor scurrying like a mouse to pick them up, rub them on his filthy smock, and then place them back upon the pile, all before looking about to see who had observed him, grinning to think his secret safe, and then repeating the farce all over again, without learning his lesson. Mr Hale mused on how he had never been very good at discovering secrets, so he was thankful that his daughter was not one to harbour any. She told him everything that was on her mind, whether it brought her joy or woe. She always had, ever since she was a little girl, and as far as he knew, she always would.

'You have a lot to contribute, Margaret, you often share your opinions and thoughts on our texts and topics.'

A sarcastic laugh erupted about the room. 'And Mr Thornton disagrees with me at every turn.'

Her father simpered to hear his daughter speak with the naivety of youth. Long may it last, thought he.

'But he enjoys it, I know he does,' he insisted. 'You can disagree with somebody, my dear, and still appreciate their point of view and feel stimulated by their conversation,' he explained, knowing all too well that his daughter always assumed that discord meant disharmony, when in fact, it was often the basis for a healthy discussion, and if one nurtured it properly, it was also the foundation of a sincere friendship.

'I have noted that Mr Thornton is always so much brighter and engaged when you are there.' What followed was a strained hiatus, after which Mr Hale quietly added, 'But in the past few weeks, he has seemed...distracted...almost disinterested, and it is not like him, not like him at all.'

Margaret looked up as she heard her father trail off, a forlorn withering to his words as the end of his sentence sagged with unmistakable sadness.

'You sound worried, Papa,' she ventured cautiously.

Mr Hale sniffed glumly, his own head bowed in solemn contemplation.

'I am afraid to say that I am. I am worried about him, *very*.'

Margaret stopped at once and frowned. Putting down her sewing, she rose from her seat and came to stand beside her father, a man who had aged considerably over the past few months alone, more so than she had seen in all her nineteen years, but then again, that was no surprise. Placing her hand on his arm, Margaret's fingers lightly curled around his sleeve and squeezed there in loving reassurance.

'Papa?' she pressed, her voice gentle and encouraging.

Mr Hale sighed. 'I may not be the most observant person, Margaret, you know I am not,' he said honestly, and she bit her lip, unable to argue, 'but I cannot help but feel there is something bothering Mr Thornton. He is...changed,' he concluded, inept to think of a more precise word.

The daughter nodded. 'People change,' she reminded him. 'I have, I think...I hope,' she affixed, thinking on how her perceptions and prejudices had been challenged since coming to Milton almost a year ago. When once she had been impetuous, inflexible in her views, and far too ready to argue, Margaret now trusted that these traits within her had been placated by maturity. Still, if only she had been more steady, more willing to listen and less eager to judge, she could have seen the worth in him, in a man who was honest and honourable to a fault, and it pained her to acknowledge how bitterly she had let him down by way of pitiful thanks.

Bobbing his head from side to side in deliberation, Mr Hale knitted his eyebrows pensively. 'Yes, people do change, that is true enough, but not like this, no. And even if they do, one would hope it is for the better, but as for Mr Thornton, he seems to have altered for the worse,' her father described regrettably. 'I fear, my dear, that all the light has gone out of him.'

Without even realising it, Margaret tightened her grip on her father's arm, her grasp tensing as her apprehension grew.

'*Tell me*,' she urged, unable to bear being kept in the dark when it came to the wellbeing of a man who had become inexplicably important to her.

He shook his head, unsure of where to start. 'He is restless, that is for sure. When he enters the house, he is always looking about him, into rooms, as if he is searching for something he is missing,' Mr Hale began, scratching his head, incapable of comprehending such peculiar behaviour, which, if he had taken the time to assiduously consider, would have become perfectly obvious.

'When he sits, I can see him looking at the door constantly, and if not there, then his head jerks up at every flutter from above. He is inattentive, his attention is always preoccupied, and he cannot seem to focus on anything. I am sorry to say that he has lost all enthusiasm for his learning, strange, since he is a natural scholar, and always found such contentment in it before. Indeed, as I was leaving the dinner party at Marlborough House, the same one you attended, Mr Thornton asked me whether he might increase the number of his lessons and come twice a week instead of once. He was most keen, I remember it clearly. But now…,' yet Mr Hale could not finish the sentence, his voice dwindling.

She waited, trying her best to be patient. '*Now*?'

There was a lengthy interval while Mr Hale thought, then, finally, he sighed again, his shoulders slumping as he settled on his conclusion.

'I think that John is sad.'

Margaret quailed, her eyes widening in distress. '*Sad*?!' she echoed.

'Yes, that is the only way I can describe it. He is…unhappy.'

She could not explain it, but she felt a surge of unrest stirring inside her, leaving her incapable of feeling anything else, Margaret's only care now was the here and now, wondering and worrying about what her father meant.

'And what do you think the cause might be?' she reflected aloud, afraid of his answer, but she had to hear it, *she had to.*

'I do not know, I honestly do not know,' Mr Hale responded truthfully, a hint of frustration to his reply to know that he was incompetent when it came to working people out.

'I wish I could ask him, but I am not adept to making such enquiries, and as for Mr Thornton, he is so very private, that I fear he would take offence and think me meddlesome. These northern men, they value their independence, and I should so hate to interfere with his. No, all I can think is that it is to do with the mill.'

'What is the matter with the mill?' she asked, a little too abruptly, trepidation taking over her manners.

'I believe it is struggling, that *he* is struggling,' Mr Hale revealed.

Margaret could hardly believe her ears. 'But how so? Mr Thornton is so very clever, so very capable, so why on earth should he be struggling? *No!*' she rebelled, unable to accept such an inference. 'I imagine that he is merely busy. He may be overwhelmed with orders at the mill and finds his time in high demand, both there and at the court. He is an important man, after all. Yes, it is most likely a matter of stress and not distress,' she went on, more to herself than anything else, trying as best she could to pacify her own reservations about his welfare.

Her father nodded blithely to hear his daughter defend Mr Thornton so fiercely.

'Perhaps, my dear, perhaps.'

Margaret was about to carry on with her sewing, but before she did, she suddenly took her father by his hands and held them close.

'I hope…I hope you have told him that we are always at his service, Papa?' she entreated. 'Mr Thornton has been so very kind to us, *all of us*, and I should hate him to think that we are ungrateful, that we do not care for him in return. I hope he considers us his friends, and therefore understands that we will always be here to offer him a helping hand, no matter how modest it may be, no matter…no matter what happens.'

Mr Hale lifted a hand and cupped his daughter's cheek. Looking into her eyes, ones which were wonderfully earnest, he bent down to leave a kiss on her forehead.

'What a lovely young lady you are, my darling dove,' he praised, using his late wife's endearment for her, thinking on how proud her mother would be to see their Margaret now, so grown up, a woman in her own right, one who was astute, rational, assured, and above all else, beneath her sometimes defiant bravado, she had a heart of gold, a caring, compassionate and courageous heart. All the same, his serious demeanour soon resumed.

'However, I am sorry to say that there is probably very little we can do. If his troubles are related to business or finance, then we neither have the expertise nor the means to assist. And if it is an affair of the heart…well,' said Mr Hale, trailing off, his attention once again absorbed by the cart that lumbered along with its unsteady swaying.

'After all, hearts, as we know, are funny things. They can be passionate. Reserved. Loyal. Vulnerable. All of these. None of these. And above all, they can be a lonely and mournful place to dwell, if one lives with a broken heart.'

Margaret swallowed thickly. Oh, yes, perhaps Mr Thornton's sadness was down to a broken heart, after all, she had not thought of that. Nevertheless, if that were the case, there was nothing she could do to help, not when he had told her that his heart was none of her concern. While it hurt Margaret to think that Mr Thornton may care for another, she knew that he deserved to know contentment, to have a home filled with love, especially at Christmas, and so, in her heart of hearts, all she wanted was for him to be happy, even if that meant she could never be, because *the future must be met, however stern and iron it be.*

Chapter Three

It Was Exactly a Week Later

It was exactly a week later that Margaret stood beside the front door of her Crampton house, pacing to and fro impatiently, something she had been doing for the last half hour, near enough wearing a hole in the rug, an oriental design acquired from the wonders of the Great Exhibition, given by Aunt Shaw to her late sister as a memento of a marvellous excursion she had been too ill to attend in person. Every few minutes, Margaret would stop and move to the mirror, slowly turning left and then right, assessing her appearance from every angle to spot any hidden blemishes of cloth or complexion that she might have missed. She had decided to wear her new dress, the one made from the fine muslin Edith had sent from India, with its cream underlay and soft pink petals that decorated the length of her arm, stitched into the gossamer lace, like sleeves of silken flowers. The cut was not terribly fashionable, but then again, neither was Margaret, so it would have to do. Besides, it was one of the few garments she owned that had not yet been tarnished by soot from the kitchen fire after helping Dixon bake and cook. Nodding resolutely, she compressed her skirts. She tidied her hair. She pinched her cheeks. She – *oh*! It was no use. Vanity was not Margaret's middle name, it never had been, so there was no point in her indulging in such empty-headed nonsense, not when he would never even notice anyway.

At long last, there was a knock at the door, and with her eyes alight with excitement, Margaret rushed to open it, just about tripping over her own feet in her frenzied haste. Only, when she did, she halted, and all at once, she felt her heart sink like a ship plunging to the bottom of the sea.

'*Oh*,' she murmured sullenly. 'It is only you.'

Before her, on the doorstep, was none other than her father, his reedy arms laden with a stack of books, the heavy bundle which overtook his hands having caused him to thump on his own door by means of his elbow, hoping there would be somebody nearby on the other side to offer assistance before the whole lot tumbled to the ground and disappeared into the snow, the ink of unread pages crying into that same carpet of white and staining it black.

'My word, Margaret, I have never seen you so animated. You looked quite giddy when you opened the door,' Mr Hale said jovially as he came in and shook himself, the sleet that had settled on his coat falling and landing on the floor as specks of white that soon dissolved into tiny puddles of water, Aunt Shaw's rug being insulted once again.

'I am pleased to see the colour return to your cheeks, my child, but you certainly gave me a fright.'

Margaret, who had been occupied in glaring resentfully at the front steps from whence he came, quickly snapped out of her self-indulgent stupor, and went to help him with his books.

'I am sorry, Papa, it is just...it is just...is Mr Thornton not coming today?' she asked distractedly, reaching up onto her tiptoes to scour the street behind him in search of a familiar face. 'It is his usual day and time.'

Her remark sounded more like a question than a statement, but it was most definitely the latter, because Margaret knew fine well that this was indeed the mill master's customary day and time, his precise day and time, to be exact, and with punctuality being a particular idiosyncrasy of his, it left her wondering where on earth he was.

'Oh no, no, he is away. Did I not say?' he commented inattentively, handing her his scarf to hang up, glad to be rid of the stifling loop of yarn wrapped around his neck, even if it were bitterly cold outside.

In the seconds that followed, Margaret could have sworn that she shrunk a whole three inches as her spirits plummeted, and she dropped back down onto the soles of her feet with a thud, a glum pout upon her face.

'*No*,' she muttered, the single word ringing out suspiciously like an accusation. 'No, you did not.'

'Well, he is. He has gone to France for business,' her father explained matter-of-factly, and Margaret felt a jolt of distress to think that Mr Thornton was travelling at this time of year. He may have been a man who was well-accustomed to braving tempestuous circumstances, but that did not seem to mollify Margaret in the least. The roads would be icy, the darkness would be dismal, and that was saying nothing for the sea, the water treacherous with the volatile waves of Neptune's realm. The Channel was but a short journey, she knew that, but Fred had told her so many frightful stories of boats being battered by storms that it was hard not to imagine the worst, and Le Havre was significantly further away than the crossing-port of Calais. Margaret could hardly bear to envisage Mr Thornton anywhere else but safe and sound here in Milton, where he belonged. She wanted him home, she wanted him to come home *now*, if not to her, then at least to the refuge of his own study and slippers, as her father would have put it.

'When will he return?' she demanded to know, rather rudely as it happens, her anxiety getting the better of her.

However, Mr Hale did not seem to notice his daughter's impertinence, which was most likely due to the fact that he was preoccupied in wondering what was for lunch, praying that Dixon had not overcooked and charred the beef once again. After all, his poor old stomach could only take so much gristle, and while he may no longer be a clergyman, he trusted that the good Lord would be sympathetic and take pity on him.

'I understand that Mr Thornton is to be away for quite some time, longer than usual. He said that he shall not be back until Christmas Eve,' was the simple answer. 'Oddly enough, that happens to be his next day with us, if we go by his usual attendance, that is, as it falls on a Thursday this year, and I have invited him, naturally, out of courtesy, and goodness knows that we would welcome his company. All the same, I very much doubt he shall come, he shall want to be with his family, I should think.'

On hearing this, Margaret shuddered. At first, she thought it was because of the cold, the door not yet closed in the wake of her disorientation, a biting breeze blowing in and snaking around her ankles. But in truth, her tremor was all down to perceiving her father refer to Mr Thornton's family, and to know that she was not counted as one of them, even though she could have been by now, because he had asked Margaret to become one of them, a Thornton, living and existing by his side, as his wife, as close a family member as one can get.

Oh, but she had not said yes, she had chosen to say no, there was that to remember.

'No, Papa!' Margaret argued, her retort so sharp that he stopped, startled, and stared at her in bewilderment. Still, this did not deter Margaret from speaking her mind.

'He *will* be here; I truly believe he will. Mr Thornton, he will not let us down,' she assured him. 'You will see your friend on Christmas Eve, I just know you will,' she promised.

Margaret wished with all her heart that she could call Mr Thornton her friend, but she held back, uncertain of whether he would consider her a friend or not. In reality, she was not convinced he ever had, but there was one thing for certain, and that was he never would now, not unless she could find a way of winning his respect and repairing their broken relationship.

But how? It felt impossible.

Not after what he saw. Not after what she did. Not after what he said.

Mr Hale laughed, a hoarse cough tickling his throat, and then he kissed his daughter on the cheek.

'Bless you, my pet, bless you,' he commended before walking away to his study.

'You know, Margaret, I sometimes think you are growing rather fond of our Mr Thornton,' he said in jest, utterly unaware of how true his words were. 'You must not let him cotton on, Heavens no, for I think it would shock him to the core, and the poor man may never recover,' he quipped, his laugh drifting into the corridor as he closed the door behind him.

Left alone once more, Margaret found herself slumping down onto the bottom step of the staircase and folding her arms. What was she supposed to do now? She had been looking forward to his visit all day, all week, even. It had been the sole focus of her interest, so now that Mr Thornton was not to come after all, everything suddenly felt insipid and meaningless. It was most unsettling. Glancing up listlessly, she saw a posy of winter flowers hanging from the ceiling, a collection that Mary Higgins had assembled for them and strung up about the house to commemorate the newcomer's first Christmas in Milton. Margaret had liked them to begin with, they were cheery and colourful, just what the Hales needed. Be that as it may, today she spied some Mistletoe berries peeking out between the bunches, and this was too much for the disappointed girl to condone, so bounding to her feet, she reached up high and snatched down one of the arrangements, catching the thorn-barbed bundle in her hands and screwing it up, not caring that it stung as the green spines scratched her.

Grumbling under her breath, Margaret trudged along the passageway and towards the kitchen in hopes of finding something to distract her, because if a childhood spent in church had taught her anything, it was that idle hands never led to any good. As she did so, she spotted the Christmas tree that stood tall and proud in the parlour. She paused and leaned against the frame as she admired it, a tender smile pursing her lips, for she was resolved to give their green-cloaked guest the attention and admiration it deserved. The Hales had not played host to a tree in a good few years, so it still filled Margaret with joy every time her eyes fell upon this most welcome addition to their humble home. Richard and Maria Hale had first taken up the tradition when the children were small, starting when their Aunt Shaw heard of the festive fad set out by the German consort, Prince Albert, a fashion she had been inspired to imitate. From then on, the Helstone parsonage had erected and adorned a tree every December without fail, that is, until the year Fred had been forced to flee England, and after that inconsolable misfortune had struck, their home had forever interred a solemn shadow of despair, the likes of which no tree possessed the enchantment to overcome. However, five days ago, when Margaret had returned from visiting the Higgins and Boucher family, she had come back to find a tree standing in their parlour, completely bare, almost as if it was always meant to be there, somehow having grown out of the floor or walls overnight, either that, or she had simply never noticed it before. She had gazed at it for some time, mystified, and more than a little awe-struck. Nevertheless, when she had asked her father, he had casually announced that it was a gift from Mr Thornton. Margaret had been taken aback by this, but he soon clarified that it was true, that Mr Thornton had thought it might cheer them up, what with this year being one of such inestimable grief. He had apparently mentioned Margaret by name, even reservedly suggesting that the loss of first her home, and then her mother, would be a considerable burden for one so young, and so, he hoped that this would help put a smile on her face.

He had been right, it had.

Not only had Mr Thornton presented them with a tree, but he had provided them with decorations, each beautiful ornament seemingly hand-picked with such considerate care, just like with the fruit he had brought in his baskets for Margaret's mother when she had been ill. Bless him, he thought of everything. He somehow knew what they needed even before they did. As for Margaret, who may have once felt her pride piqued by such a familiar and forward gesture from Mr Thornton, a mere pupil of her father's, she had not thought twice about accepting his offering with immense gratitude. And so, over the past five days, she had spent many a jolly hour sprucing it, and now, all she could hope was that he too would like it when he saw it, that it would likewise put a smile on his stern face, one she had rarely seen etched with any expression other than a scowl, his smiles rare, especially these days. *Margaret liked this smile; it was the first thing she had admired in this new friend of her father's; and the opposition of character, shown in all these details of appearance she had just been noticing, seemed to explain the attraction they evidently felt towards each other.* Or, that is, an attraction he had once felt for her, not that he did anymore, even if she found the thought of him more attractive with every passing day that they were divided by their mistakes and misunderstandings.

Continuing along to the kitchen in a state of apathy, the kind that is typical of those who are disheartened, Margaret came to sit on the long wooden bench by the table, even if her mind was somewhere else entirely. At first, she paid no heed to Dixon sitting opposite her, peeling carrots and eyeing the young mistress with a critical eye. With a muffled grouse as she sucked her teeth, the maid did not approve of all this moping about that Miss Margaret was doing these days. It was most unlike her, and it was a pointless pursuit, since sulking never got anyone anywhere. And what was she doing all trussed up in her best day dress, one might ask? It was not as if there was anything remarkable happening today, there was no anticipation of company, nor indeed any plans for celebrations or commemorations to warrant her wearing something special. She knew one thing for sure, and it was that a fancy frock like that had no place in a kitchen. Huffing, Dixon half fretted that the girl was taking after her mother with all this pining, but she doubted it, given that Mrs Hale, God rest her soul, had been a fragile creature, whereas her daughter, by contrast, *huh*, that hoity-toity madam was made of sterner stuff, so she would soon perk up, mark her words. Unable to abide the silence, not to mention being unnerved by the way that Margaret was staring off into the distance with a wistful expression, Dixon ventured a comment, one which she had assumed would be acceptable.

'I am relieved *that man* will not be coming today,' she said after a while, in that off-hand way of hers.

Margaret, who had been playing inattentively with some scraps of cabbage and kale, froze and seethed at the maid, her eyes glinting with icy ire.

'I sincerely hope you are not referring to Mr Thornton, Dixon,' she replied, a prickly warning to her words.

'I most certainly am, Miss,' the servant retorted without so much as a blush to show for her insolence. 'I cannot imagine what the master was thinking of, having the likes of him traipsing in here. I do not care how wealthy he is, nor how fine his clothes or house may be, no amount of artificial politeness or sipping tea in our drawing room will ever take away the fact that he is a dirty, lowly tradesman. And to think he is treating the likes of you as his equal —'

'That is enough!'

By now, Margaret had leapt to her feet, and she was glowering at Dixon, her face red with an aggrieved anger that raged so hotly, it would surely ignite her, burning her to a cinder like a match. Dixon got such a fright that she flinched, the kitchen knife flying out of her hand and clattering on the paved floor.

'I never, – *never*, want to hear you speak of Mr Thornton in that way again! Do you hear?!' Margaret ordered. 'He has been so very kind to us since we came here, even when he has no need to, and even though we can offer him no advantage in return.'

'No advantage?!' Dixon scoffed. 'What? To mingle with a genteel family of birth and breeding? He being no more than a common hawker in a smart Wellesley.'

Margaret could feel her blood boiling. 'I do not know which accusation to dispute first. To begin with, Mr Thornton is not just a common hawker, and even if he were, that is no crime. I will remind you that he is an educated man, a man who is intelligent and proficient in what he does.'

'Bah!' the servant jeered, her fists kneading a mound of dough on the table before her.

'He has had no education that I know of. And what has he to show for himself, hmm? A mill? Nasty, filthy place,' Dixon sneered.

'Yes, it is true that a mill may not be what you and I are used to,' Margaret conceded, rather reluctantly. 'And I speak for myself when I say that a factory floor feels worlds away from Helstone with its beautiful fields, or London with its grand architecture, but that does not mean it is not a place to be valued in its own right. I must profess, when I first saw it, when I first laid my eyes on Marlborough Mills, I was mesmerised by it,' she confessed, thinking how she had been fascinated by this world of swirling white. It had assaulted her senses, this strange beast that roared with its noisy machines and spinning looms. Going there that day, it had been a rude awakening for her, and now Margaret could not put it out of her mind, she could never forget it, for it had left such an impression upon her, and oddly enough, she did not resent it, but felt a strange sort of reassurance to think that it was now part of her, even if she never stepped foot in there again. Then, of course, there *he* had been, standing on the scaffold, high above it all, a powerful presence, a striking and rather stirring image to behold. Still, little had she known then what he would come to mean to her, this man, this master, this Mr Thornton, of whom she had cast off and cared nothing for, all because of her senseless pride and prejudice. Suppressing a clogging lump in her throat, Margaret continued with her defence of the accused.

'You must remember that he is not merely a tradesman, but a master. From what I am told, Mr Thornton is hailed as the most successful businessman in Milton, if not the county. I know the other masters look up to him, even envy him, and he is considerably younger than them all. He is evidently accomplished in everything he puts his mind to, his achievements applauded by all who know him. He is respectable, and he is respected. Does that in itself not attest to his abilities?'

'I do not know about this northern lot, but their standards are not the same as ours,' Dixon asserted, thrusting her nose into the air. 'As the mistress said herself, they're only interested in money, that is what they eat, and that is what they breathe, along with their vile smoke. They are a dissimilar kind of people, distinct from us in every sense. They care nothing for morals or manners hereabouts. Why, to think that they would be so bold as to revolt and go on strike, saying nothing for rioting and throwing stones at a woman!' she puffed, her face turning a shade of burgundy and coming out in blotches at the indignation of it all.

As she heard her speak, Margaret lifted a quaking hand to her head and gently grazed the spot where her scar still lurked, a mark of mortification that would never go away, an emblem of her own reckless errors and all the trouble that it had provoked from that day forth. One may be forgiven at this point for being perplexed by this extraordinary exchange between the two women, wondering why Dixon would risk being so brazen and Margaret so tolerant. However, it would be reasonable to suppose that both women were testing the boundaries of their altered relationship, figuring out where they each stood, and where the other stood in turn.

'No, you'd do well to listen to me, young Miss, he will be more than pleased to have his feet under the table here, mixing with the likes of Mr Hale, a true gentleman who has never dirtied his hands by a day's manual labour in his life, a man who can introduce him to some proper men of refinement.'

'Mr Thornton *is* a true gentleman, Dixon, the truest that ever lived.'

'Is he now?' she said with a sceptical grunt. 'From what I understand, he is a man with a scandalous past,' Dixon interjected, her eyes narrowed with a grim soberness that left Margaret in no doubt as to what she meant, that she had dared to touch upon a most grave subject indeed.

Margaret felt a shiver creep up her spine and drag its claws down her back, like the ghostly talons of death itself.

'*Dixon*,' she whispered, her words thick with tension, 'that is hardly his fault.'

The maid leaned her head to the side. 'Perhaps not,' she accepted, 'but it is still a disgrace and a sin.'

At this, Margaret stood up and began to stride back and forth, beset by an aching restlessness. She was about to remind Dixon that the Hales themselves were not immune to ignominy. What about Fred? His actions, albeit honourable ones, had led him to be branded as a mutineer, condemned to live in exile for the rest of his life unless he wanted to end that very same life on the gallows. But no, there was no point, because there was no arguing with Dixon when it came to her beloved Frederick, the golden boy who could do no wrong in her eyes, unlike Margaret, the girl she had always scolded for being too obstinate and opinionated when she should have sat quietly and acted like a docile creature, a biddable doll with no mind of her own. In any case, they were not talking about Fred, but about Joh — Mr Thornton.

'Whatever actions his father took, we should not judge. We do not understand fully what happened, and more importantly, we ought to pity him for feeling so hopeless as to do such a thing. To leave his wife and children like that, to say goodbye from this world, the wretched man must have been so lost and alone – so afraid! And as for his son,' Margaret persisted, her voice growing stronger and more resilient, 'he deserves our praise. I shudder to imagine it. A child, on the brink of manhood, with his whole future ahead of him, having it snatched away most cruelly, and then to be hurled into the abyss of poverty and obscurity. It must have been a heavy burden for a boy to carry, and as a young man, I believe he worked tirelessly to provide for his family and to reclaim their rightful place in society. Not only that, but he was dedicated to paying off his father's debts, even when those persons owed had no hope of recompense. He gave up everything, and without complaint, he denied his own wants, and he did what was right by others. He suffered his own Hell, I think, and he is a better man for it. A more dependable, careful, thoughtful, empathetic man. And for that, Dixon, I think he is perhaps the most endearing person I have ever known. Moreover, I cannot think of anyone of my acquaintance who could have endured such trials with half the nobility of character as Mr Thornton has done, and still continues to do to this day,' Margaret championed, her eyes shining with pride.

It occurred to her for the first time how difficult it all must have been for Mrs Thornton. While Margaret did not agree with the way the mother guarded her son like a baby chick that needed her incessant protection, lest it try and fly the nest, fall, and break its wings, never appreciating that he was a grown man who was already soaring, she now understood the anxiety this solitary parent evidently harboured in her heart. To have witnessed him being battered and bruised by the callousness of life, and being defenceless to help him, save as a constant source of encouragement, then it must have left Mrs Thornton feeling a sense of mistrust and aversion towards any suspicion of hindrance to his health and happiness, wishing to safeguard his welfare at all costs, including shielding his heart from any woman who may be careless enough to break it.

'And now, I wish him well. He deserves to be happy, he has earnt that right, even if the right to happiness is not something that ought to be earned.'

However, Dixon was not convinced.

'That might be the case,' she acknowledged, 'but it only serves to prove my point. He is tarnished by his past and all he lost as a consequence, so he comes here because he wants to learn how to become a man of significance, and Mr Hale, even if he were only a country clergyman, is as much a man of consequence as that tradesman will likely ever meet in this heathen backwater.'

'You are wrong to call it a backwater,' Margaret challenged. 'From what I understand, towns like Milton are at the heart of our nation, driving it forward with astounding energy and enterprise, guiding us into a modern age, one of ideals and industry. The people here are hard-working, independent and rightly proud of their self-determination, and for that, I admire them.'

'That may be true, Miss,' Dixon allowed, 'but that does not mean they do not wish to be better, and how are they to learn to be better? From their betters, that's how,' she went on, nodding across the table to Margaret. 'They can be as vigorous as they like up here, with all their new-fangled, polluted wealth, but they will always lack the inherent respectability of the south.'

'Those things do not matter here, Dixon, as well you know. Milton is a different place, with different people, who have different ideals. They care little for the tenets of the south, and what is more, I commend them for it. Besides, I am quite sure that even if they did value such petty trivialities, Mr Thornton would still not mind them himself. No, he has no interest in a person's personage, so long as they are conscientious and earnest, rendering them worthy of his good opinion,' Margaret upheld.

The young lady then cast her eyes to the floor demurely, a paleness bleaching her countenance. Who was she to speak so vehemently of honesty when she herself had been so shamefully dishonest? It was true, Mr Thornton did prize the virtues of sincerity and integrity, discounting those without such qualities, but what was correspondingly true, was that Margaret herself could not claim to be so righteous in her character. Therefore, it went without saying that Mr Thornton could never respect her, and nor, it would seem, forgive her.

'And I will remind you that we are not so high and mighty as you might imagine. Do you think Milton sees us as impressive or influential? I assure you that they do not. For are we not in reduced circumstances?' she asked, pointing a finger at their confined living quarters.

'We are hardly the richest or most esteemed people here. We do not hold grand dinner parties or balls. We do not have gentry banging down our door to call upon us, and we never did before. Good gracious, Dixon, we can hardly afford a servant to help you, so I must do it myself, the daughter of one of your precious Beresfords,' Margaret reminded her, throwing her hands up in the air at the ridiculousness of it all.

Dixon herself was knocked for six. Well, she never! To be spoken to like that, and in her own kitchen! Oh, she knew that Miss Margaret had a temper, she always had, even as a little girl, but by Jove, she had never made a scene like this before. And all because of her charitable and wholly misdirected interest in a worthless cotton merchant. There was one thing for sure, and that was that this dreadful place was going to her head, and the sooner she was sent off to marry a London gent, such as that nice Mr Lennox, the better.

Thinking on this thread, Dixon tactlessly added, 'I will tell you one thing, though, I cannot imagine anyone wanting to be his wife.'

If Dixon had been paying attention, she would have seen the woman opposite her holding back the tears that welled behind her eyes and glazed them in a glistening mist. Sitting back down, Margaret laid a hand over her face and repressed a whimper, her shoulders shuddering with the weight of the emotions that unsettled her awakened heart. Taking care to hide behind her palm, Margaret scoured it across her face to wipe away the rivers of water that trickled down and stained her cheeks. With her hand sneaking into the right pocket of her dress, Margaret caressed something that lay concealed within, a pair of somethings, to be exact. Something black. Something leather. Something that was not hers to possess, but she kept them close, all the same.

'Oh, I do not know,' she breathed into the fingers which muffled her mouth, her lips kissing the creases of her joints. Her oration was so soft, that Dixon could not hear her, her words a private soliloquy, a monologue of tortured thoughts as the full magnitude of her puerility dawned on her. She now appreciated what she had been offered for the first time, really appreciated it, and what was more, she realised what she had lost, probably forever.

'I think any woman who would not want him must be a very silly girl!' Margaret observed with a sorrowful laugh as she sniffed, the maid still too distracted to take any notice of her.

'I dare say there's many a woman makes as sad a mistake as I have done, and only finds it out too late.'

Then, turning back to face the stove where Dixon stood, tipping over a plate of turnips and watching as they fell into a bubbling pot, Margaret waited for her to come back. When she did, Margaret smiled at her with forgiveness.

'Dixon,' she started, reaching across the table and taking the maid's hand in her own and patting it fondly, 'it is of no matter if you and I cannot agree to like Mr Thornton. It is not possible for everyone to approve of everyone else and see their merits. However, there is one resolute fact which you are overlooking, one which is unshakable, no matter what you and I may think,' Margaret insisted, and Dixon put down her rolling pin to lean forwards in anticipation, the fervency in the lass' face too compelling to disregard.

'Mr Thornton *was,* without question, wonderfully generous to mother, you know he was,' she championed, her voice calm once more, and the maid looked shamefaced to have forgotten it. The new mistress of the house was well aware of how much her mother had loved Dixon. She had been more like a friend than a servant, a devoted companion who had been with her since before her marriage, steadfast in her loyalty throughout every new chapter of their parallel lives. Nevertheless, even if Mrs Hale had never, and probably would never, have come to entirely understand or appreciate Mr Thornton and all he stood for, Margaret knew that it would have pained her mother to hear him disparaged in this house, particularly after he himself had been such a faithful friend to them all.

'What is more, all this talk of gentlemen. What is a gentleman, anyway? Who is to say? You and I may both be right, and we may both be wrong. But I think it is of no consequence, because, after all, it does not matter whether Mr Thornton is a gentleman or not, for I believe that he is something far more important besides.'

'And what might that be, then?' Dixon asked, her nose scrunched up in doubt.

Margaret smiled once more, a tender, knowing smile.

'He is, by very definition, a *good* man,' she said. 'And, at the end of the day, that is all that matters. So, please, Dixon, do not speak of Mr Thornton in that way again. I cannot bear for him to come here and not to be shown every civility and consideration he so justly deserves. It is hurtful. Not only to him, but to m –,' Margaret bit down on her tongue. 'Just...*please.*'

Once she had finished her speech, Margaret resumed playing with her vegetable husks, her demeanour now one of gentle mildness once again. As Dixon watched her, she saw the young miss shiftlessly pick up her father's scarf and run it between her fingers, the girl so befuddled by her let-down this evening, that she had forgotten to return it to its peg.

'I will say one thing for him,' began Dixon, rubbing her flour-coated hands on her apron, 'he will need to get himself a scarf soon. Either that, or he will freeze to death.'

Margaret glanced up in confusion. '*Father*?'

'No, Mr Thornton,' the maid corrected. 'He has been without one these past four weeks or more. I heard him say so to the master. He gave it to a child, or so he said, one of the children in his factory who hardly had a stitch on his body and was walking home in the snow. He has not yet got around to acquiring a new one. And as for his gloves −'

'*His gloves*?!' Margaret repeated, nearly jumping out of her seat.

'Yes, he lost those too, some time ago, from what I understand. I tell you this, for a man who is supposed to be so careful with everything, he has a funny way of mislaying all his clothes,' Dixon remarked, once again braving a criticism.

'But it is a shame for him, poor soul. He may be a northerner, and from what I should think, he will have thicker skin than you and me, but to go out in this fearsome cold with no scarf and gloves, it is unthinkable!' she tutted, her maternal side never failing to win her over.

'I heard him say that he shall get a new one by and by, but he wants a blue one. And not just any blue, mind you, it has to be a cloudy blue, a sort of pale grey. It is his favourite colour, apparently. Odd, is it not, for a man to be so exact about such a thing?' she mused to herself.

Margaret nodded, but as she noted her reflection in a copper pot, she paused, the colour of her eyes catching the light and causing her to squint before quickly looking away.

Could it be...? No, no, a coincidence, surely.

Nibbling her lip, Margaret began to drum her fingers on the table as Dixon ambled off to stir the stew. It was at this moment that an idea came to her, and Margaret snapped her fingers.

Yes!

She knew what she would do to show Mr Thornton that she cared about him, to prove to him that his friendship meant the world to her, and with two weeks to go until Christmas Eve, she would have plenty of time to see her plan through with conviction.

Chapter Four

You Fool!

John Thornton trudged through the snow like a plough, fighting against the storm of snowflakes that attempted to both throng and stab him.

'Humbug!'

He tried his darnedest to ignore the biting sting as the cold of the slush that caked his legs stole up him like an assailant, first encasing his toes, and then stealing inch by inch up towards the landmark of his knees. Muttering some regrettably ungentlemanly words under his breath, John continued on, each step he took more dogged than the last, the blood that pumped to his thighs and calves being fortified by an added dose of determination.

He would go there! He would get there! He would get to see her!

Yes, even if it was the last thing he did, even if it killed him, John *would* see her tonight.

He scoffed noisily at his own moronic idiocy. This was insanity! He had been away for three weeks, three drawn-out, weary, fruitless weeks, and this was John's first day back in Milton. Needless to say, there were a multitude of tasks that required his urgent attention at the mill; letters, machinery repairs, invoices, and goodness knows what that he had to look over if everything was to resume a status of normality under its commander's efficient routine. He had been imprudent to put off returning this long, to avoid Milton and all it contained, but he had told himself that it was necessary, that it would be beneficial for his forthcoming trade plans, that it would lead to better things, and not only that, but John had also strived to indoctrinate himself into believing that a little time, a little distance, they would help him get over...

Sigh.

At any rate, it was not just about business, because what of his family? John knew that he ought to be spending tonight with his mother and sister, the two of them having been denied his company for longer than was standard, not that Fanny would mind, of course, she would hardly have noticed that he was gone, or if she had, she would have delighted in it, her joy only subsiding when she saw him walk back through the door. As for his mother, she would be anxious for her son to remain at home and get some rest. In fact, she had been pestering him all afternoon about staying in and regaining his strength, the shadows under his eyes and sag of his typically imposing stance enough to tell her that he was weakened, if not in body, then certainly in spirit. Nonetheless, he had resisted her entreaty, and much to his mother's annoyance, John had insisted that he would be going out tonight, no matter what. He was set on it, inflexible man that he was, one who was not easily bent by opposition or perturbed by obstacles. If he were, then he would have never made it this far in life, his steadiness and perseverance intrinsic to his character, the fundamental foundation of his ability to not just survive in the face of misfortune, but to prosper. In light of this, there was one thing that his absence had taught him, and it was that when John Thornton had settled on something, whether it be a commitment of his time, his intellect, his purse, his industry, or indeed, his heart, he would be unfaltering in his loyalty until the bitter end.

So that was that. He *would* love her, whether she wanted his love or not.

John halted in the middle of the street, and there, he leaned against a lamppost, and growled in despair like a wounded beast. Unfolding his arms, which had been huddled in front of him to stop his fingers from turning blue, he lifted one of his gloveless hands to his face and drew it down from top to bottom in jaded despondency.

'Oh, John, John, John!' he muttered. 'What are you doing? *You fool!*'

On stopping, his legs began to feel their fatigue, and they flagged beneath him, causing the mill master to at first sway, and then slump against the post, the hard, ice-smeared metal smacking into his back and proffering him some comradely support, as well as a hefty clout of scornful ridicule for being such a buffoon. Appearing like something akin to a Dickensian ne'er-do-well who was guilty of mafficking, he was grateful that there was nobody around, for if there had been, they would have lingered and gawked at him, speculating as to whether he was drunk, before promptly judging him for his sorry state. Then again, perhaps he was intoxicated, but not on drink, rather, on love, that sweet and sickly potion inebriating every thread of his person, both exhilarating and afflicting the individual fibres of his soul, drugging him like a spell that was too powerful, too perfect in its pain, to break.

John knew that he should not go to the Hales. On his journey back from France, first on the boat, then on the train, then in the carriage, he had been afforded plenty of time to give himself a thorough talking to, impressing upon himself that he should not attend his usual lesson tonight. He would make his excuses, for he had numerous and legitimate ones, and undoubtedly Mr Hale would understand perfectly, unassuming friend that he was. For Heaven's sake! It was Christmas Eve, after all, a time for family, a time for staying at home beside the fire with a glass of brandy, when a man could congratulate himself on all he had achieved over the past year.

John gritted his teeth and scowled.

Of course, in his case, what had he actually achieved?

Letting his eyes slowly wander up from the blanket of snow that covered the ground, John's gaze fell upon a window directly opposite him, on the other side of the street. Even though the thick curtains were partially drawn, he could still glimpse the clandestine haven inside, peeking through the thin tear in the veil of their privacy that had been carelessly left agape, and through that narrow slit, he spied a family: father, mother, child. The three of them were certainly a merry sight, one which simultaneously filled John with hope and hate.

Why hate, one might ask?

If truth be told, John did not hate anybody, not really. Yes, it would be fair to say that there were many people he mildly disliked, mainly because he considered them either loud, licentious or lazy, three words, three shortcomings, that he could not abide, but as for hate, no, that was a strong word, even for a man of such strong convictions. Nevertheless, it was true that what he saw tonight filled the master with profound hatred. It was because John despised them for being so happy. How could it be that others boasted this effortless ability to find serenity, yet for him, it was an allusive dream? As John observed them from a distance, he felt his heart cry to witness the way the wife smiled adoringly at her husband, the look of wholesome faith in her eyes as he bent down to kiss her, their relationship not one of mistrust and animosity, but of unequivocal respect and reverence.

God! What a year it had been! A year of revelations. A year that had unravelled him.

Never before in all his twenty-nine years had John thought about taking a wife and having children of his own. He was too busy for such things, and if he were honest, John was always afraid that something would go wrong, meaning that he would be unable to provide for them, so he was best not dragging them into his life, one tainted with a history of failure and humiliation. No, a mother and sister were enough female company for him, more than enough, or at least, that had been so, up until a year ago, when his priorities had unexpectedly and abruptly changed, when his ordered world had been shaken asunder by the sight of a pretty face.

John could have watched them for hours, lost in an introspective haze, but his attention was snatched away as the child ran across his vision, galloping about gaily, his little legs jumping and skipping as he savoured the magic of this night. The man then picked up his son, and pulling his wife close, the three of them were secured in his protective embrace, a jumble of arms wrapping around each other in unreserved love.

After that, John had to look away. It was too much to bear, too great a grief for his heart to harbour, thinking, knowing, that he would never experience such pure contentment, not as a husband, nor as a father. No, he was doomed to spend the remainder of his days as plain, insufferable, unlovable John Thornton.

Master. Magistrate. Nothing. Nobody.

'Oh, Margaret,' he whispered into the wind, the unscrupulous breeze whirling his words around and spitting them back in his face like a hawk of mockery.

'That could have been us,' he breathed, thinking that if she had said yes six months ago, they could have been married by now, and possibly even blessed with the knowledge that they were expecting their first child. But it was not to be, because she had said no, and so, that was that.

Finally, John gave in and continued on, leaving the unnamed family behind to enjoy their harmonious night in peace, far away from the contempt of his loneliness. As he walked further across town, John's mind turned to think on matters that were so unfriendly in their dejection, that the surrounding coldness no longer bothered his bones by comparison. Instead, he tried to occupy his mind more pleasantly. John hoped that Margaret had liked the tree. He had chosen it carefully, ensuring that it was the very best he could find, not counting having parted with a pretty penny for his efforts. He was not sure if it was a step too far, an overfamiliar offering that a London gentleman would never have presumed to give. John had deliberated about it for some days, but on the afternoon that he had left for Dover, he had finally given in and ordered the tree for the Crampton house, meticulously taking into account its restricted proportions. It was after determining that he was not a man to be concerned about niggles in regard to social etiquette, so long as his intentions were honourable, which, of course, they were, that John had concluded that it was the right thing to do. And what was more, he and Margaret had been through so much together, a private affair of the heart, a bloody battle of admiration and apathy that was unknown to almost everybody around them, that he felt justified in extending this gift to her on the first Yuletide since they had met, the first Christmas that they could have been, should have been, man and wife.

Approaching the graveyard that sat high above the city, John found himself brusquely stopping again, and with his eyes raised to the heavens, he sighed once more. John was not entirely sure whether he believed in God, not after everything he had been through as a young man cast into the callous world. He had experienced hardship, and he had suffered heartache, and so, he often wondered whether God really existed out with the mind of man, or whether he had simply given up and gone away, assigning humanity to writhe in the fire of its own gradual and agonising downfall. Still, one thing was for sure, and that was that God had been cruel to Margaret this year. John would not call himself a particularly sympathetic person, but he could at least grasp when someone was careworn. In fact, he was often referred to as a surprisingly understanding justice of the peace, appreciating that extenuating circumstances, such as the sequences of deprivation and violence, often left people feeling alone or afraid, making lawlessness appear like an attractive answer, a radical act that would resolve their problems, when in reality, it only sought to aggravate them. Still, even with this insight, John held fast to the principle that struggle was a natural part of life, that in order to survive and thrive, one must walk through the flames of adversity in order to be moulded, to be bent into shape, and to come out stronger than before, ready to brave the future with an armour of mettle. Be that as it may, despite himself, John could not help but feel deeply sorry for Margaret. She had been through so much, sweet creature, and what was worse, was that he was helpless to help her. As a master and a magistrate, for better or for worse, he had at least some modest influence in the lives of others, but when it came to her, what was he to Margaret? Nothing, that's what. Grudgingly, John knew only too well that he was no relation of hers, nor was he an old and trusted friend, so he had no alternative but to stand back and watch while her world collapsed around her, and all the while, there she would stand in the midst of her sorrow, defiant and dignified to the last.

Darling Margaret. Fierce Margaret. Remarkable Margaret.

She had been forced to leave her Helstone home, her paradise, saying goodbye to her London family and friends, and come here, to Milton, a town marred by voracity and grime, somewhere she most assuredly did not belong. Thenceforth, after all that, after all the upheaval she had endured, bearing it with such rousing heroism, she had lost her mother. John felt a wretched sensation stab at his heart, and he scowled at the snow, just like he scowled at everything else these days. Yes, he knew all too well of the trials of loss. With sober recollection, he reflected on the grief that death could bring, the devastation it could wreak if it were defiled by disgrace, a trauma that his dear Margaret had at least been spared. Then again, had she not been dealt a more unfair hand than he ever had? It was true that John had known poverty, it had been his companion for many years, the shadow of which he could swear still stalked him, a phantom that would not leave him alone, and it made him shudder every time he sensed its unwelcome lurking, threatening to drag him back into its pit of privation, a trench that he now felt too old and too tired to dig his way out of all over again. In spite of this, while the changes in his social position had been more severe than Margaret's, more shaming by far, at least he had been able to stay in Milton, with his own people, finding security in his familiar surroundings. However, in her case, Margaret had been obliged to wave goodbye not only to a parent, but a house, a financial sense of stability, a landscape, a drove of family members, and her rightful place in society. And in that lay the crux of the matter. For Margaret, it had been worse, infinitely worse, and for that, John could not forgive God for turning his back on her, something he himself would never do, no matter what she had done to him in return.

Reaching the inn that lay just a street or two away from the Hale's, John strolled past it, and as he did so, a stranger, a blonde-haired man staggered out, and when he saw him, the master's fist tightened into a ball so taut, that the nimble bones of his fingers began to grind and crack.

That bast –

No! John would not degrade himself by being so uncouth, the scoundrel did not deserve such consideration.

Oh, but *he was!* He was that word.

That was one of the reasons why John had agreed in advance not to come tonight. What if *he* was there? As he had already observed, Christmas was a time for family, so would it not be natural for Margaret's young man to join in the festivities and rejoice in ushering in the dawn of Christmas Day with the woman he lov –

No! Stop it! John did not know that the man loved her, nor that Margaret returned his affections, no matter how damming the evidence might be. Yes, this had been one reason why John had felt it best that he should keep away, in case the man had been there, and then what? He discovered him to be a crook and was forced to deal with the villain to protect Margaret's honour from this gal-sneaker? Or worse, that he turned out to be a perfectly decent gentleman, despite his reckless and selfish actions which had resulted in Margaret being out late at night, rendering her vulnerable to both attack of body and accusation of character? To be sure, it could be that under all that thoughtless foolhardiness, he was a good man, a man who warranted her devotion. After all, John could not conceive Mr Hale permitting his only child to associate with and attach herself to an inappropriate lover. But then again, Mr Hale might not know. He did not know everything. He did not know that his pupil had fallen in love with his daughter and asked her, implored her, for her hand in marriage. However, this impasse did not help him, because it brought John no closer to deciphering Margaret's relationship with the man from the station, the one she had embraced under the cloak of darkness, as if they had something to hide, gazing at him as she did with unquestionable love.

It was now, plagued by the thought of such an undesirable conclusion, that John shivered, his neck tilting unconsciously as he scoured his naked skin against the fur lining of his coat, begging it to be compassionate and impart some warmth. He needed to keep his head if he wanted to remain sane, so it went without saying that the stock on which it sat should be kept alert, lest the nerves within freeze and obstruct, the blood in his veins hardening into clotted rivers of ice, unable to flow, causing him to lose his wits altogether.

The truth was that John was both ashamed and afraid. He could not help but suspect that Margaret was avoiding him, in fact, he was sure of it. He had attended four weeks of lessons in the shade of her half-presence, her absence manifest, her refusal to see him unbearably cruel and crushing. Only, he deserved it, deep down, he knew that he had well and truly earned her displeasure. He had hurt her with his words, ones he could not take back, no matter how sorely he wished there was a way to reverse his blunder and recover what little semblance of respect and regard she had held for him.

Nonetheless, John told himself that Margaret was just as much at fault as he. She had started this war between them, she had fired the inaugural shot, not he. It had begun when the southern beauty had initially arrived in the town, just under a year ago. Her self-assured ways were undeniably amiable, her unabashed independence admirable, rare qualities that had attracted John to her from the beginning. Nevertheless, her arrogance and preconceptions, these faults that were born of youth and inexperience, they unfortunately served her ill, clouding her opinion of him and compelling Margaret to set herself up in defiance against him and all John stood for.

Then he had proposed, albeit without thinking things through, he realised that now, but she had been the one to be harsh, condemning his feelings and humiliating his hopes, reducing them to something laughable and pathetic, denouncing every facet of his proud character. After that, she had been cold with him, although, perhaps that was nothing more than a lack of poise on Margaret's part, the woman unable to understand how to be around him, how to act, how to manage the onslaught of his affection, especially when it was offered with such cloak and dagger like secrecy and suppression. There had even been days when John had left her presence in dismay, wondering what on earth he was playing at, raking over his gruff and uneasy manners, so it was no wonder she was probably similarly confused by his unpredictable bearing. While he should have been patient, proving to Margaret that he could be relied upon, that he was a steady bet as a contender for her hand, he instead gave in to his precarious passions. By means of his feet, John had allowed his temper to carry him away from his beloved more than once, never once smiling at her as he marched off, never once admitting how he truly felt, his discourtesy, his querulousness, they each eclipsed the acute agony that tore his soul to shreds. Love was surely supposed to be consistent, but in John's experience, it was downright chaotic, even if his devotion to Margaret was forever constant, as constant as the stars. After that, in the fracas of their furious clash of wills and wants, there had been Outwood, the event that had altered everything, devastating all that remained of his frail hope. He had seen Margaret with her man, and then she had lied, not just to John, but to the law, and in doing so, she had wounded him twice. Her falsehood had proven to him that not only was she capable of deceit, a wrongdoing he would never before have imagined accusing Margaret of, but that at the same time, she had committed the even more heinous crime of loving another, and by this offence, she had hurt John more than she would ever know, more than he would ever show.

During the tense weeks that had followed his proposal and then her duplicity, Margaret had never once recoiled into the shadows and removed herself from his sight. No, she had faced him. She had been bold, insolent, even, showing him that she did not reproach herself, that while she took absolute responsibility for her decisions and her conduct, Margaret felt no blame, perhaps even no remorse. Then it had happened, the very thing John had dreaded happening, and at the same time, dared to happen.

'Is Miss Hale so remarkable for truth?'

Chapter Five

But Why Was She Hiding?

God! How those careless words still rang in his ears like a clanging bell.

John remembered it all too well. *The moment he had* spoken that malicious line of petulant hostility, *he could have bitten his tongue out. What was he? And why should he stab her with her shame in* that *way? How evil he had been* that night; *possessed by ill-humour at being detained so long from her; irritated by the mention of some name, because he thought it belonged to a more successful lover; ill-tempered because he had been unable to cope, with a light heart, against one who was trying, by gay and careless speeches, to make the evening pass pleasantly away, — the kind old friend to all parties, whose manner by this time might be well known to Mr Thornton, who had been acquainted with him for many years.*

And then to speak to Margaret as he had done!

He had hidden his hurt poorly, his attempt to repress it rendering it more potent than ever, almost like a fermenting venom that festered within him, and for this senseless reason alone, John had lashed out when last he saw her, on that evening when he had taken tea with Mr Hale and Mr Bell.

She had not risen to leave the room, as she had done in former days, when his abruptness or his temper had annoyed her. She sat quite still, after the first momentary glance of grieved surprise, that made her eyes look like some child's who has met with an unexpected rebuff; they slowly dilated into mournful, reproachful sadness; and then they fell, and she bent over her work, and did not speak again. But he could not help looking at her, and he saw a sigh tremble over her body, as if she quivered in some unwonted chill. He gave short sharp answers; he was uneasy and cross, unable to discern between jest and earnest; anxious only for a look, a word of hers, before which to prostrate himself in penitent humility. But she neither looked nor spoke. Her round taper fingers flew in and out of her sewing, as steadily and swiftly as if that were the business of her life. She could not care for him, he thought, or else the passionate fervour of his wish would have forced her to raise those eyes, if but for an instant, to read the late repentance in his. He could have struck her before he left, in order that by some strange overt act of rudeness, he might earn the privilege of telling her the remorse that gnawed at his heart. It was well that the long walk in the open air wound up that *evening for him. It sobered him back into grave resolution, that henceforth he would see as little of her as possible, — since the very sight of that face arid form, the very sounds of that voice (like the soft winds of pure melody) had such power to move him from his balance.*

Well, whether he had wished to be estranged from her or not, it had happened, she had made sure of it.

John cussed himself.

What an unholy night that had been! How dare he have spoken to Margaret in such an offhand way?! Curse that blasted temper of his! She had been shocked and saddened by his targeted outburst, he could see that as plain as day on his darling's sweet face, and it had wounded her in a way that he did not even know he was capable of. Lord knows that this revelation had upset John punitively, to think himself skilled in injuring her so, savage beast that he was. How could she ever love him when he could hurt her like that? John had crossed a line that night, and from that moment on, everything had changed between them. Up until then, Margaret had at least tolerated his presence, doing her best to overlook and even pacify the palpable tension between them, to pardon his smouldering resentment, and to be as polite as she could.

But not now.

John had been desperate to speak with Margaret after his insensitive mistake, to tell her how sorry he was, but she had not seen him to the door as she usually did, he had been denied that sacred privilege as a means of peculiar punishment, no doubt, so he had not been granted the opportunity to beg her pardon. He had half decided to come and call upon her the next day, and then the next, and so it went on, but he made petty excuses for himself, blaming the mill for keeping him tied to his desk. The long and short of it was that John had been pigeon-livered and held back until the following week, resolved that he would get a chance to be alone with Margaret on the occasion of his next lesson and plead her forgiveness then, telling her the blunt truth about how he felt, and why he had been such a fiend.

But she had not been there…

Not that night, or any night since.

It was like she was gone, spirited away, displaced and dismissed from his life, but never, - *never*, from his heart.

Her patience with him had reached its limits and come to an abrupt end, and he knew this because, for four weeks since, she had not been there. That is, she *had* been there, but she had not been *there*. She was in the house, that much was certain, his keen senses being sharpened, attuned to tracking her with the precision of a hunter. He may only have known her for nigh-on twelve months, but John had familiarised himself with every aspect of Margaret's character, along with the particularities of her movement of body and tenancies of mindset, a study that had been at first unintentional, but by now, it had become almost obsessional. With great frustration, he could hear her moving on the upper floor, detecting sudden and fleeting bursts of activity, then all would go still, like a millpond, and he realised that she was trying to be quiet and not draw attention to herself, even if by doing so, she was, by paradoxical contrast, making herself more conspicuous than ever.

In other words, Margaret was hiding from him.

On his last visit, three weeks ago, John was about to leave, but then he had heard a creak from above, and a silhouette had been cast about the place, almost as if somebody were leaning over him. Looking up quickly, he could have sworn that he saw a face, a pair of eyes surveying him intently from between the railings. There had been a fitful vibration of light, suggesting something had moved swiftly, and so he had impatiently watched and waited, praying that she would make herself known. But then there was nothing, no clue as to what it was that had disturbed him, and so, he gave up his futile search, accepting that another day, another week would pass without seeing her, the master being once again denied her most charming and coveted company.

But why was she hiding?

Could it be that her father spoke the truth and that Margaret was ill? John flinched. Lord, he hoped not. It was not that he believed Mr Hale capable of dishonesty, but it could be that Margaret had told him that she was unwell, seeing as it would be one of the few acceptable reasons that would account for her non-attendance, and so, her father had simply trusted her. John could not bring himself to think of Margaret being in poor health, and the notion had caused him to get up and go to fetch the doctor time and time again, but on every occasion, Mr Hale had promised him that things were not as bad as all that, and he had felt unable to argue. Consequently, John had been obliged to settle down and take his tutor's word that the woman they both loved more than life itself, was not in any danger. At first, John could believe this excuse. Margaret had been busy, too busy, looking after her father, the house, and every other wretch she came across, so it was no wonder that she was plausibly a little worn out. However, then the second week had come, and then the third, and finally, the fourth, and it was then that John knew for sure that she was evading him.

But again, why?

John needed to think about this rationally.

Margaret was not one to hide herself away. She was too audacious for that, so there had to be a darn good reason. At this point, John felt all the colour weep from his cheeks when he considered the one possibility that had been haunting him for some time, ever since he had awoken on the ship to Le Havre in cold sweats as a nightmare overtook him and persecuted his mind.

Was it conceivable that Margaret was with child?

John had woken up one night and near enough cried out, an image plaguing his subconscious in which Margaret cradled her growing belly, a dream he had once welcomed with longing, but not this, not this distorted and corrupted likeness of her slender figure swelling with the life of another man's seed.

He shook his head violently.

No!

She may have had a dalliance with that young man, but Margaret would never have given herself to him, not like that, not before she was married. But then John suddenly felt horribly sick. What if she had not given herself at all? What if he had taken what was not rightfully his? What if she had not even tendered her love, but had been forced? Without knowing what he was doing, John lifted his clenched fist and slammed it against a wall, ignoring the pain as the bricks cut into his knuckles and bruised them, thin trickles of blood running furiously along his hand and seeping into each overlapping stream with a sting. John barely noticed, merely taking out his handkerchief and cleaning up the mess.

It was time he faced facts.

Whether he liked it or not, it was possible that Margaret was with child, however it had come about. That would explain why she was concealing herself, keeping stealthily out of sight, and it would explain why her health was compromised. It was most likely that her father did not even know, that would vindicate his unperturbed conscious and conduct. He was presumably in the dark, for Margaret may have covered it well, or not yet been far along enough for it to be obvious, not if one were not deliberately looking for the signs of pregnancy. John refused to believe that her father did know and was playing his pupil like a fiddle, the very thought of such betrayal from a man he cared for as a father enough to break his heart all over again.

Well, if it were true, John would not disown Margaret. No, he would stay loyal to her, even going so far as to offer for her once more, vowing to look after her and her baby. He would even allow the illegitimate mite to take on his own name, instinctively choosing to care for it as if it were his babe, even if it were obvious to everybody that he could not be the father, not only because of timing, but because the child did not resemble him in the slightest. John would do the right thing by her, and he could do nothing more than that, so if need be, he would propose again, despite accepting that any agreement would not come from a place of love, but of necessity on her part, the thought of disgrace and destitution being just marginally worse than the thought of marriage to him. However, John would not let himself dwell on such dark thoughts of an uncertain future. He had no evidence to support his unspeakable theory, and so, for now, he would try his best to banish it from his mind. What was more, knowing Margaret, or what he thought he knew of Margaret, it was unlikely to be true, and besides, there was another reason which made far more sense, and if John were wholly honest with himself, he knew it to be the real cause of her refusal to see him.

She simply did not love him.

Well! He had known what love was – a sharp pang, a fierce experience, in the midst of whose flames he was struggling! but, through that furnace he would fight his way out into the serenity of middle age, - all the richer and more human for having known this great passion.

When he eventually reached the street on which the Hale's home was tucked away inconspicuously in a corner, John did not slow down, but continued at his punishing pace, all too aware that his courage derived from his grit, and if he stalled, he may never make it at

all, just like a machine starved of energy and coming
to a standstill. At long last, when he arrived at the foot
of their home, John finally allowed himself the right to
stop. Good Lord! How his limbs ached. He had not
appreciated how ruthlessly he was driving himself
forward. He was about to walk up the steps, but before
he did, John gave way to his longings, and he
bestowed upon himself one small indulgence, one
moment of brief relief in which his self-denial was
overthrown from its throne. Letting his eyes train up
from the fissured pavement, John looked towards her
bedroom window. The onlooker knew it was her
window, he had seen her there before, many months
ago, when he was first becoming acquainted with the
Hales. He had peered up casually, without reason, or
so he had told himself, and John's captivated eyes had
stopped still as he spied Margaret by chance. There
was nothing indecent about what he saw; she was
simply standing there, re-arranging her hair, twirling
from side to side as she flattened the creases in her
dress, all acts which suggested that it was Margaret's
own boudoir. No, there was nothing improper about
what he beheld, but all the same, his observation
should not have lingered and become a stare, but he
could not help it, he was fascinated, and from that
point on, John had known that he no longer wanted to
be a spectator in Margaret's life, watching and
admiring her from afar. He wanted more. He wanted,
needed, to be close to her, with her, to be intimately
part of her world.

John had intentionally looked up at the same spot
three weeks ago when he had begrudgingly left that
humble home, hoping beyond hope that she would be

there, searching for him, just as desperately as he searched for her, but it was not to be. Nevertheless, John had been certain that he had glimpsed a movement out of the corner of his eye. The curtain, it had quivered, he was sure of it, but then all was still once again, and so he had departed, his heart heavy with an aching need to see her.

As John stole a glance up at her private realm tonight, the curtain was once again drawn back fully, and there was a light on the windowsill, bathing the room in an ethereal glow. Even so, there was nobody there, and John made ready to resume his march up to the door, but then out of nowhere, something changed, and a figure approached the scene. John's breath caught in his throat as his head bucked up, and his mouth fell open as he regarded that hallowed window, all his pent-up passion sparking his senses.

It was her!

Good God! It really was her!

Just like that, Margaret came into view, and John hardly knew where to look. She glided towards the glass, towards a table that must have sat before it, and there she began to fold something and place it on a sheet of brown parcel paper. Her cheeks were radiant, her lips parted, almost like she was singing. She was adorned in a gown of the most striking red, a green band around her waist, colours which spoke of Christmas cheer. At first, John was busy taking in the loveliness of her appearance, marvelling at her carefree expression, but he was soon distracted by the sight of her laughing, something he had never seen before, and it was the most beautiful thing to behold. The cause of her amusement was adorably entertaining. Margaret was grappling with a line of ribbon, the unruly twine having got itself wrapped around her wrists and arms, and so now she was struggling to untangle herself. John found himself laughing too at her childlike farcicality, a sound that had become foreign to him in recent months. It was strangely comforting to see her befuddled. Margaret, this clever, confident woman, who was always so sure of herself, never being discomposed, yet here she was, all in a tizzy, and John liked it, for it was reassuring to know that she was human, after all.

Then, all of a sudden, she looked up.

The seconds that passed next, for seconds they would have been, felt like hours. Margaret momentarily glanced in his direction, and then she stilled as her wandering eyes met his. She simply froze; she did not blush, or frown, or even attempt to scurry off. With wide eyes and a slanted head, just like a little bird, she stayed there, matching his gaze with unswerving focus. John's heart was beating faster than it was surely safe for it to do so. He knew he could look away, even retreat with some semblance of respectability, but he did not, because something inside him refused to tear itself away from her. He had hungered for her for so long, you see, and now that he had her in his sights, John would be a fool to ever look away again. Instead, the two of them stared at each other, and finally, Margaret lifted a hand to the glass, and there, she pressed her fingers against it, her digits twitching slightly, as if to shyly wave. If he were not so mistrusting of his own worth, John could have vowed that there was a flicker of yearning in her eyes as her hand reached out to him. At last, she took her fingers away, and this time, Margaret bent them towards her, beckoning her visitor to come hither, and what was more, she smiled at him in broad, wholehearted welcome, all before she disappeared from view, like an apparition invented by his most sacrosanct desires.

John gulped.

Well, there was one thing for certain.

She had *never* looked at him that way before.

Chapter Six

Nowhere I Would
Rather Be

Despite it being only a few feet between where he stood on the pavement and the Hale's front door, it would not be an overstatement to say that John near enough sprinted that immeasurably short distance, taking strides rather than steps as he hurried towards the house and all the hope that its four consecrated walls promised. The fatigue in his legs had miraculously vanished, and instead of feeling emotionally bled, he was alive with an agitated exhilaration that made him as giddy as a schoolboy. When he reached the door, John knocked upon it eagerly, the thump of his fist sounding dubiously thuggish with its booming thud, advertising his whereabouts to the whole of Milton. Nevertheless, his vigour, albeit raucous, did not come from a place of aggression, but of uncontainable excitement. Standing there, John must have looked like a puppy as he bounced up and down on the balls of his feet, the new-found and pent-up energy that fizzed inside him proving difficult to restrain. He was in half a mind to take hold of the handle and push the door open of his own initiative, but John quickly took hold of himself instead, reminding himself that love, no matter how passionate it may be, was no excuse for bad manners.

However, John did not have to wait long, stewing hotly in his pot of fretful expectation, because only a few moments later, he heard the plod of footsteps on the other side. John could feel the blood rushing throughout him, directing itself to every nook and cranny of his substantial body, feeding his flexing muscles with the red fuel of vitality, shovelling it like coal into his veins. He was like a greyhound about to be set free from his pen at the races, and he was ready, ready to charge inside the very instant the gate was unlocked, and he was at last at liberty to chase after what he wanted.

Just like that, the door opened, and much to his surprise, it was not a surly Dixon who met him, threatening to turn her enemy away and clobber John with a rolling pin if he dared contest her, but Mr Hale himself. The master of the house wore a vague expression at first as he surveyed his caller, his faculties dimmed by the lateness of the hour and the darkness of the street on which John stood like a displaced statue. Still, his countenance soon transformed into one of heartfelt greeting as the realisation of who had arrived dawned on him.

'Ah, John, here you are!' Mr Hale acknowledged merrily, a tad taken aback, as Mr Hale, a man who could not boast the sharpest of memories, had almost forgotten that they were due a visitor at all this evening.

'Welcome, my good man, welcome!' he hailed as he stepped back and threw his arm out in the direction of the hallway, shepherding John inside from the harsh northern air.

John breathed a sigh of relief to have been invited in, even if the hard part was yet to come. He had half wondered whether Mr Hale might have overlooked the fact that tonight was their usual day for meeting, and what with it being Christmas and all, the pupil may very well have been sent away with his tail between his legs, wandering home like a lost soul, the very same eager puppy being denied his Yuletide treat, the chance to see his mistress.

'Good evening, Mr Hale,' John replied breathlessly as he marched over the threshold with a brisk step, overtaken by a queer superstition that if he did not cross that marked line swiftly enough, the door would slam closed in his face, and as if by some rotten curse, he would be unable to get in, rendering both the Hale home and the Hale daughter barred to him forever.

'Thank you for having me,' he added with delayed civility as he took off his coat and hat, laying them down on a nearby table, since the thought of handing them to Mr Hale to hang up somehow seemed inappropriate, even if he was not entirely sure why. As he commenced his inspection, the sight of a pair of out-of-place knitting needles courted his interest, and they made John look twice with a curious blink, speculating as to what on earth they were doing there, and even more intriguingly, why they were not employed with any knitting, a single strand of blue wool the only evidence remaining to suggest they had been busy at all.

Mr Hale waved his hand about affably. 'Nonsense!' said he. 'We are merely flattered that you could find the time to come and join us tonight. I know you have only just arrived back from your travels, and you must surely have a great deal to see to, and I am certain that you will be wanting to spend time with your family at Christmas.'

John smiled, a small, private smile. 'Believe me, sir, there is nowhere I would rather be,' he confessed, disregarding the pang he felt to think that she could have been his family by now, the very nearest and dearest of family members, if only she had said yes.

It was at this point that the caller took the convenient opportunity to look about him. Now that he was indoors, he had matters to attend to, and as a man who was not work-shy, John thought it best to get on with his urgent task directly. With single-minded tenacity, and eyes as sharp as flints, John restlessly scanned the lower floor, the parlour and the stairs, hoping to detect a movement, an evanescent shadow, a sign that they were not alone. However, much to his mounting frustration, nothing flitted across his elevated eyeline, nothing caught his penetrating scrutiny; not a maid, not a maiden, not a mouse.

Grumble.

Snorting impatiently, John transferred his attention to the poky passageway that led to the kitchen. He yearned for some tell-tale din to echo from that quarter, such as the beating of dough against a table, the shrill whistling of a kettle boiling on the stove, or sweetest of all, the sound of someone humming a comely tune. If he strained his lugs, then he could by chance heed the dainty pitter-patter of light feet, and the pacing of slipper shoes from some unspecified corner of the Crampton house, but their presence was both muffled and fleeting, leaving John's supposition unsubstantiated. John tried to distinguish even the feeblest of noises drifting down the corridor or the stairs, but no resonance came his way; not a shuffle, not a sniffle, not a sigh.

Growl.

He stood stock-still and let his surroundings flood his senses. Surely he must be able to *uncover something*. A sight, a touch, a sound, a taste, a smell…Come on! – *anything* would do! All he had were two knitting needles and a string of wool, and what meaning could they possibly hope to harvest? However, unfortunately, regrettably, his wits came back with a discouraging report, informing him that there was no —

'Kind of you to say,' Mr Hale interjected, interrupting his visitor's anxious search, 'but will your mother and sister not be missing you tonight? I do feel terribly responsible for having taken you away from them, particularly when they have been without you for so long.'

John allowed himself a brusque laugh as he thrust his hands into his pockets, his fingers only just waking up from being numbed lifeless by the cold, and the sensation of their reawakening was causing his skin to sting and smart, a burning that was more raw than his masculine pride was ready to admit.

'I doubt they will mind my absence too much,' he said truthfully, his head tipping backwards at an unnatural angle so that he could inspect the floor above, since he was not so much occupied with those who lived at his own house, but rather, those who lived here, or that is, a specific someone. The thought of this irked him momentarily, and he frowned crossly, because if John had his way, that person would be living at his house, with him, permitting him to spontaneously see them whenever he liked, morning, noon or night. Nevertheless, as ill-fate would have it, that was not how things were, so he had no alternative other than to spend whatever precious-little leisure he had with them here, or that is, try to. John heaved a heavy sigh when no indication of their presence greeted his ears, and he soon turned his fickle focus back to his host.

'They are to dine with the Latimers this evening, and then join a party there for the masters and their wives. I hear they have a great deal of food and games planned, so that will almost certainly regale them both. I should think they will consider it a welcome change from my dull company,' John affixed, all too aware that his sister was overjoyed to have the chance to indulge in the elegance of a festive party, giving her a coveted opportunity to throw on her finest frock and both dance and gossip the night away, the non-attendance of her elder, lacklustre brother being the icing on top of her Christmas cake.

'Oh, dear! Now I really do feel guilty,' Mr Hale wavered, his cheerful features drooping, affecting his wrinkles to defect from being upward creases to downward ones. He reproached himself to think that in his loneliness, he had been selfish and coerced his friend in coming all this way just to keep him company. The Hales lived in unpretentious simplicity, and their humble celebration this evening could never hope to compare with a grand congregation of his peers, the kind of fashionable event a smart young man about town would surely be eager to attend.

'I fear you shall find us a modest gathering tonight, dear boy, just the three of us: myself, you and Margaret,' he confessed frankly, exhaling loudly through his nose, by contrast, making a show of his sincere apology. 'I promise you, as welcome as you are, if you wished to leave, we would not be slighted in the least.' Mr Hale's oration faltered as he said this, for while he meant every word, he would be more sorry than he could say to see his esteemed friend depart.

Nonetheless, John merely shook his head with uncompromising resolve.

'I can assure you, Mr Hale, *this* is precisely what I want.'

It was true, he would much rather be here, and not just because of whom he might see, but because John categorically detested parties. He abhorred the effort of getting trussed up and being forced to engage in mindless small-talk with a horde of inebriated men and infatuated women. Somebody would be constantly trying to steal him away, whether it be for a dance or a conversation about trade or the law, and so John found the circus that was socialising to be tiresome. He was a man, after all, not a performing ape, a pitiable creature who was forced to entertain others as they crowded around to demand that he satisfy their acquisitive fascination. John had anticipated that if he had gone tonight, then he would have been swarmed by ladies who tried to trap him under a stem of mistletoe, their fathers or husbands equally exasperating as they pressed him for every monotonous detail of his business dealings abroad. No, no, peace and quiet were what John longed for, and where better to find it than in the refuge that was the Hale's?

He sniffed sentimentally as he brooded on this, on how he had spent the past fifteen years searching wretchedly for a place to call home after he had lost his own. He had thought he would find it in the mill or in the courthouse, realms of stability and order. But what a fool he had been to look in such taciturn places that cared nothing for him in return. It was only now, by sheer accident, or perhaps sheer luck, that John had finally discovered his home. Not his literal home, of course, but his spiritual home, and he was not ashamed to admit that he was prepared to do all he could to stay.

Thinking on this, John added reassuringly, 'Being here, sir, with you, *with both of you*, it promises to be the perfect Christmas Eve.'

Then, bending his head down to examine his shoes, he faintly whispered, '*almost*,' since it was true, John could not be happier, or that is, he could, if only she would come to him. Better yet, John wished with all his might that she would run into his tender embrace, melting in his arms as they wrapped themselves tightly around her, just like he had dreamt many a lonely night, and there he could hold her, kiss her, tell her he loved her, and better still, better by far, hear her utter those sweet words of faithful affection in return.

While John was indulging in this fanciful fiction, Mr Hale was mulling over his own. He had not perceived

John's private mutterings, his satisfaction at hearing that his favourite pupil was to stay after all had left him insensible to anything else, and with a tear of joy welling in his mawkish eye, he murmured, 'Well, as I say, we are honoured.'

Veering round, and looking towards the stairs, Mr Hale suddenly called out: '*Margaret!*' and John felt his heart stir to hear that name mentioned, his three favourite syllables like a melody composed by his very own soul. It had been uttered so unexpectedly, and without any ceremony, that John felt thrown by it, as if its power had whipped a rug out from beneath his feet, knocking him off balance, and he held onto the table for support. Her name was so singular, so superior, that it ought to be proclaimed formally every time it was mouthed, like royalty being announced before they entered a room.

'Margaret, dearest, look who is here, it is Mr Thornton,' her father proclaimed.

John shuffled gauchely and dug his nails into the wood of the table, scratching out thin lines in the panelling like the scrapes of a wild animal, physical proof of the intensity of his hunger for the one he awaited restlessly. Stooping in embarrassment, John was overwhelmed by a curdled mood of discontent when he realised that the sound of his own name could never bring her as much joy as hers did him. John was so stark, so uninspired, so short, whereas Margaret, *well*, it encompassed everything that was good in this meaningless world. Still, his head soon shot up again when he heard the most unexpected sound imaginable, so astonishing that he deemed it high time he cleared out his ears. What came next, was a call from high above, up the stairs, and it was one full of warmth and cheer, both sentiments ringing with the celestial chorus of sincerity.

'Coming, Father, coming!'

Her voice was lyrical in its liveliness, and John's eyes stared in unconcealed awe as he saw Margaret appear before him like a vision, making him wonder whether he was in fact some madman who was driven so crazed by longing that his delirious mind was concocting things. She was halfway up the stairs, tilting over the banister so that they could see her. Margaret was smiling as she regarded them, a look of authentic happiness on her face. It was not surprising that John found himself fighting to breathe, and he seriously worried that if he could not swallow enough oxygen, he might keel over and collapse on the floor at her feet, and what a ridiculous spectacle that would make. His chest grew tight as his heart swelled at the thought of being close to her again after all these weeks. He could feel his whole body reacting, groaning into life, as if it had been asleep during the interlude of their disaffection. The hairs on his arms bristled. His fingers jerked. His throat convulsed. He must have looked wild, but he did not give a damn, not when he was about to see his darling girl again. John no longer cared what had transpired between them, all that mattered was being here and being near her, because despite any anger or jealousy that he might be wrestling with, none of that burdensome pessimism outweighed how much he had missed Margaret. Consequently, John was hardly aware of Mr Hale talking, the gentleman drivelling on about something or nothing, the master too absorbed with impatiently awaiting Margaret's arrival to concern himself with anything else. With an impatient quickening of his pulse, he watched as she descended the stairs, her every step as graceful as the gliding of an angel. Her admirer only frowned once, and this was when she vanished for a brief moment from his sight, hidden by a bend in the staircase that impeded his view. However, while he was inwardly cursing the blind spot for concealing his favourite person in all the world, John was momentarily distracted when he heard Mr Hale say something odd, very odd indeed, and it made him blink, whirl round, and glower at his tutor in blatant bewilderment.

'What did you say?' he checked, unsure of his own state of mind, his ears most definitely playing tricks on him, all those nights being out at sea and exposed to the blustery winds that brawled with their time-old battle between the shores of England and France having temporarily deafened him, not to forget having spent years living and working beside machines that rumbled like a boisterous beast with a bellyache.

'I was just saying that I am only sorry that you will be denied the company of Miss Latimer,' Mr Hale repeated, a little more stridently this time to ensure that he was heard.

'I understand that she is a fine young lady, and if you forgive my overfamiliarity, I am led to believe that it may not be long before I am to congratulate you,' he tallied with a skewwhiff wink, not that Mr Hale had ever quite grasped how to wink, not being a winking man himself.

John's face fell. '*Congratulate me?*' he repeated, dumbstruck.

Mr Hale chortled. He knew his pupil was a reserved man, but really, there was no need for him to be so reticent amongst friends. 'Why, yes, on your engagement to Miss Latimer.'

Chapter Seven

The Mislaid Teaspoon

It was true that John Thornton was a remarkably clever man, his mind as fast and fertile as any, affording him the useful ability to process information at a quicker rate than most. All the same, this admission from Mr Hale was more than he could fathom. *Where on earth had he heard that he was to be engaged?* John was about to reply, to bark a baffled series of questions and retorts, first demanding to know who had fed his friend this heinous lie, shortly followed by a most explicit denial of the false allegation. However, unfortunately for him, John did not have the chance, as before he could open his mouth, Mr Hale spoke again.

'Oh, excellent! Here you are, my dear!' the father said, greeting his daughter and clapping his hands jovially with a single smack that echoed. John spun round to see Margaret walking towards them, his gaze tracking her until she stood wonderfully close to him, so close that he could feel the heat radiating from her body, one he tried his best not to stare at, since its generous curves had the ability to turn his mind to mince, rendering him ungentlemanly as he gawked at her with poorly disguised desire. She looked so delightfully lovely, as always. How was it possible that one woman could be this arresting? It was surely impossible, and one thing was for certain, and that was that it was unfair. How could a man be expected to be in control of himself when he was around such a divine creature? John felt sure that Margaret was some sort of enchantress, because that was the only plausible explanation, even if it were not the most rational. The most incongruous detail was that John had never been truly attracted to a woman before. Yes, he had considered the occasional girl handsome enough, but he had barely noticed any of the women who paraded themselves before him, no matter how relentlessly they tried to filch his attention and claim his affection, these overripe bit o' raspberries that were nothing more than fakes in finery. On the other hand, when it came to Margaret, John was spellbound, and he had been, ever since the first day they had met. Could it be that years of disinterest in the opposite sex had meant that he now had a reserve of bottled-up avarice to release? Meaning that when he finally found himself charmed by a woman, John could not help but be captivated by every inch of her beautiful being?

However, getting back to the point, it was fair to say that John's joy was soon made uneasy when he detected the patent shift in her comportment as she approached. Where she had been spirited a few moments before, Margaret was now apathetic, her happy attitude disquietingly overcast. She stood before him in meek silence, her head hung low, her hands fidgeting before her, all the healthy pigment drained from her previously rosy complexion.

'Look who it is!' Mr Hale declared, gesturing towards John as if his daughter was an imbecile, as if she had not seen him a dozen times before. 'And he came, just like you said he would.'

Nevertheless, instead of glancing up to greet his gaze, Margaret's eyes remained fixed upon the floor, her lids heavy, as if weighed down by some unknown sadness.

'Miss Hale,' John rasped, initiating their discourse, his throat hoarse as he struggled to speak in her presence.

John had never claimed to possess a way with words. He was articulate enough for the likes of Milton folk, a species who were frank with their phrases and blunt with their gist, their time always harried, never their own, rendering conversation rudimentary, and only entered into when strictly necessary, opposed to being an art form that was taught in the south. In contrast, when it came to Margaret, she deserved so much more. John knew that she ought to be showered with poetry, with pretty verses that dripped from her lover's lips with dulcet adoration. But alas, he was not gifted with a silver tongue, what with having a sharp one in its place, so all he could manage were curt snippets of dialogue, each one usually punctuated by a disarray of glowers and grunts. It was a combination that must have made him appear like a boor to her, this refined woman of elegance who could simultaneously soothe and scold his soul with her mouth, a delectable trove that he yearned to plunder with his own.

'It is good to see you again,' he added, his words as honest as honest gets, yet neither Mr nor Miss Hale would ever know how sincerely he meant them.

Margaret nodded ever so slightly, her small hands clasped before her in doleful solemnity, almost as if she were standing before him to be admonished. Her submissive bearing was puzzling to him, not to mention distressing, but for the life of him, John could not work out the cause of her subdued mood.

'Good evening, Mr Thornton,' she whispered back after a while, her typically imperious voice so faint that he would almost believe she had lost it entirely.

And then no more was said.

To say that the next two hours that passed were the most tense of John's life, would not be an exaggeration in the least. He had endured many uncomfortable encounters over the years; such a drawback could not be side-stepped when he was both a prominent master and magistrate. Nevertheless, despite his experience with the menace that was known as social uneasiness, John could never quite seem to prepare himself for the overwrought awkwardness that arose when he was around Margaret. As a self-governing sort of fellow, he was used to being his own, sole commander, to being measured by his speeches and deeds, allowing him to demonstrate to those who surrounded him that he had earned his reputation for being both intelligent and authoritative. In spite of this, whenever he was with Margaret, John found that he was useless, abysmally so, a right foozler who was incapable of forming a coherent sentence, unable to say or do anything other than scowl or sulk, all because he was too darned frustrated that he did not have the same overwhelming effect on her.

Still, even though John could concede that he and Margaret had shared countless self-conscious meetings over the past year, nothing compared to tonight. After she had convened with her father and his pupil by the front door, Mr Hale had ushered them all upstairs to enjoy some tea and cake beside a hearty fire. Margaret had accompanied them dutifully, but while she had descended the stairs with energy and enthusiasm, she ascended them with listless lethargy. It was almost as if she had lost interest in the whole night and would rather not be part of it. John had sensed himself constantly turning his head furtively to look at her as she trailed behind them, if only to check that she was still there. When they entered the drawing room, it was a reprieve to find that she did indeed join them, that is, eventually. This interval of uncertainty had been the longest ten seconds of his life, waiting for her to catch up with them, wondering if she would make her excuses and continue up to her bedroom. In the end, much to his relief, Margaret did no such thing, but rather, she sat down in a chair at the other end of the room, and there, the lady of the house took up her sewing. Disregarding his initial gladness, John was far from pleased with how the situation was progressing, because he did not like it, not one bit. For a start, the seat she had chosen was so far away, that it may as well have been at the other side of the county, the country, even, he north, she south, the two of them to be eternally divided. There were plenty of other spots to nestle herself, all much closer to him, but she had opted to remove herself from him and erect a barrier of cold indifference known as distance between the pair of them. What was more, the demonstration of her sewing implied that she had no intention of joining in their conversation tonight, and John was near enough ready to get up and storm off, declaring that if she were not to talk, then it was pointless, since he had no interest in listening to anything that was said unless it came expressly from her. Even so, John tried to reason with himself. She was here. That was a start, at least. It was a vast improvement on past weeks, stagnant and suffocating as they had been, even if tonight did not offer all he wanted, for now, anyway. Still, he would wait. John may have been well-schooled in self-denial, but the second most practised string to his fiddle was forbearance. Yes, he would let her be, and do his best just to be grateful that Margaret was here at all.

Over the next two hours, Mr Hale talked about this and that, the gentleman far more garrulous than John had known him to be for some time, and while he was delighted to see his tutor's former verve restored after his months of vanquished grief, he felt guilty for not paying him due consideration. John tried to be attentive, he really did, but it was hard when his awareness was constantly devoted towards minding what Margaret was up to. For the first forty minutes, she did not even glance up from her work, not once. She kept her head bent diligently over her sewing, and John was mesmerised by how skilfully her fingers floated back and forth as they pulled the needle through the fabric of whatever it was she was embroidering. However, as homely as this was for him to watch, it would not do. It was just like it had been on his last visit, or that is, the last visit on which she had graced him with her presence, and they had sat together in this room, and John would not stand for it. She had been like this before, strangely timid, and John hated to see Margaret thus, not this woman who ought not to be confined to a corner in silence, but one who should be the heart and soul of whatever room she was in, governing it with her wit and wisdom. He was so accustomed to having her challenge him, to hear her blistering remarks of admonishment or abhorrence channelled his way, that John found he sorely missed her chastisement. *Ha!* It was ironic. He had tried his hardest to win her over for months, craving so much as a morsel of approval, and now, all John wanted was for Margaret to scold him like she used to.

Turning in on himself, John ignored Mr Hale's comments about the latest pamphlets on philosophical discourse that had been published, choosing instead to try and work out the cause of Margaret's altered disposition. She had most definitely been agreeable enough when he had arrived not four and forty minutes before. If his memory was correct, she had been singing and laughing in her bedroom, he had seen her with his own eyes, ardent eyes that had watched her with more attentiveness than was right and proper. After that, she had hurried down the stairs to join them, her voice high in its genuine gusto. So then, what had happened to make her so forlorn? Allowing his paranoid thoughts to cloud his judgement, John even began to worry that Margaret had not realised it was him who was visiting, that she had assumed it was somebody else, perhaps her lover from the train station. Then, when she finally came face-to-face with her companion for the evening, she had felt cheated and disenchanted, leaving her miserable with her second-rate consolation-prize. Indeed, it was conceivable that Margaret had mistaken him for somebody else. A tall man in a hat could be confused for another man of a similar, nondescript variety. John's heart sank to think such an unhappy thought, but then he soon pushed it aside as common sense annulled his mistrust.

No, that was not possible. While John appreciated that he knew Margaret's face and figure better than she did his, given that he had made an infatuated study of her every infinitesimal inch, that is, those that were not frustratingly concealed by her clothing, it was still logical to infer that she would be able to distinguish him from any other individual. Surely Margaret knew him well enough to distinguish John from any other man she met. For pity's sake, he had held her in his arms on the day of the riot, her petite body pressed against his solid frame, her nose scraping his own, their hot breaths mingling in the tight space that separated their lips, a marginal gap that grew ever closer as they had spun in circles as one in their dizzy dance of terror, fearing for the safety of one another. She knew him! She knew his face. John refused to accept any contradiction on the matter. And there was not only that. They had watched each other intently not half an hour previous, their gazes lingering in a suspended daze, and if John were not so doubtful of his own worth in her estimation, he could have sworn an oath in court that he had witnessed a light in Margaret's eyes when she had noticed him standing in the street on his arrival. She had spotted him. Recognised him. Smiled at him. And then invited him inside. All of that had happened, it most indisputably had, and nobody would ever discourage him from clinging to this fact, or persuade him otherwise. What was more, Mr Hale had called out John's name to her, letting his daughter know that it was the mill master who had come to call upon them this Christmas Eve, and she had heard him, she had replied in acknowledgement.

So what had changed?

Pondering on this, John lifted his teacup to his mouth and primed himself to take a sip of refreshing liquid to nourish his senses with a jolt of warm inspiration, the fusion of spices undertaking to invigorate his wits. But as he did this, he glowered to discover that his cup was empty, and so he lowered his arm in tacit frustration. He was just about to stand up and fetch some tea for himself, what with it being an informal occasion that would allow for such familiarity, but then an idea came to him. With the edge of his lip curling mischievously, John picked up his spoon, and with a deft flick of his wrist, he threw it across the floor, and there it landed, just a few paces away from her feet.

His trick worked a treat.

All at once, Margaret looked up with a startle, her eyes landing upon the mislaid teaspoon with a quizzical expression. She glanced first at it, then at John, and the cords of his soul thrummed and twitched to at last be able to look into her eyes, those blue orbs that were the most soothing shade, so precise in their perfection, that no artist could ever recreate it with his paint palette. She could do that, work him like a puppet on a string, and while John could never allow himself to ever be conquered by another man, he willingly submitted himself to her mercy.

Margaret continued to inspect the spoon upon the floor, but she made no effort to stand and retrieve it, and John revered her for this. While many women would be deferential, servitude was not in her nature, her character far too stately to permit her to stoop so low as to oblige John by picking up after him like a mother does for her child. Margaret was a caring person, and while she would gladly bend and scrape to help a needy soul, John knew that it would take a great deal to convince her that a mill master required, or rather, deserved, her consideration. Instead, she folded her hands on her lap regally, and she narrowed her eyes to him in defiance, daring him to get up and fetch it himself. Needless to say that John sprang out of his chair like he had just been booted from it, his over eagerness excruciatingly plain for all to see. Kneeling, he picked it up and held it out to her. It was a peculiar act. John had no need to bend, his sprightly limbs were well-oiled enough for him to be able to crouch to collect the mislaid artefact, this prop in his theatrical performance, but for some reason, he wanted to do more than that, he wanted to make a greater show of himself. Bowing before her on bended knee was, to John, a man of chivalry, like a knight lowering himself before his lady, and as absurd as he may appear, lessened in both body and dignity in the Hale's drawing room holding a silver spoon, it felt absolutely right.

As she studied him with an air of discreet astonishment, Margaret could not help but smirk, a slight snort escaping her nose as she giggled, and it was the most beguiling sound he had ever heard, even if he knew it had not been consciously intended for his amusement. However, she soon regained her composure, and standing, Margaret took the spoon from him, and much to John's regret, their fingers did not brush when she did so, for she was careful to ensure that the tip of her dainty digits remained several inches away from his in modest partition, lest they accidentally encounter one another, sending intoxicating ripples throughout them both. With him still kneeling before her, Margaret walked around their visitor like he was nothing more than an inconsequential obstacle in her path, and she continued to the small table upon which the tea things were laid without comment.

Left alone and neglected, not to forget feeling very much like a court jester, John rose to his feet, straightened his jacket, and returned to his chair, pretending that he had not just behaved like an abominable twit in front of the woman he loved. Nevertheless, thankfully for John, the designated table was in fact situated deliciously near to his armchair, so without having to make a mockery of himself twice, he was allotted a top-ticket seat in the fascinating demonstration that was Margaret's tea pouring. He watched in carefully disciplined awe as Margaret picked up and put down first a teapot, then a cup, then a saucer, and then a set of tongs, reminding him of how, on the first time he had seen her perform this uncomplicated yet calming ritual, he had longed to take her fingers and use them like delicate pincers, even if he had never been one for sugar before. Letting his eyes rake over her, John could not refrain from admiring her like a portrait, a liberty he took rather too often, much to his niggling shame. Her dress really was exquisite to behold. He was so used to seeing Margaret in muted colours of browns and creams, but this cloth, this cut, they could not have been more different. Although John had always respected her unassuming tastes, approving of their unadorned simplicity, it was novel to be able to admire her in something bolder, more befitting of her character. It was red, a deep, wine red, with a hint of cherry-hue blended in to give it a lightsome sheen. The sleeves were tight and tapered to her shoulders and arms, creating a structured poise with material that moved down and fitted snugly around her waist, elongating it until the skirts fanned out at her hips, the design conceiving a most pleasing shape. Around her middle, was tied a thick, green ribbon, its ends coiling teasingly as they hung about her impishly. When

Margaret twisted to manage her task, John grinned as these same tails swayed and swished, and it took every ounce of self-discipline he possessed not to reach out and grab them, allowing him to tug at her sash and pull her towards him playfully. John often thought about the ways in which he and Margaret would flirt if they could, the pair of them descending into childishness as these two serious-minded people gave way to their youthful light-heartedness.

Yes, as John eyed her thoroughly, he could not help but approve.

As he did this, he found himself smiling in peaceful relief. Ah, so she was not with child, then. Or that is, she could be, theoretically, especially if she had met with her man from the station since that night, but the contour of her slender figure said otherwise, the lack of a swelling bump testament to her intact virginity. Well, that was something, he supposed. John had never truly believed it to be to the contrary, not in his heart of hearts that still trusted Margaret's honour implicitly, but all the same, it was a weight off his troubled mind. John continued to stare at her midriff indelicately for goodness knows how long, as his judicious eyes confirmed his theory. It was only when he sensed her gaze upon him that he peered up, and there he saw Margaret watching him, a furious blush to her cheeks to see the way he gawked at her and grinned to himself with satisfaction. Heartily ashamed, John removed his attention from her at once and chose instead to pick at an invisible thread on the sleeve of his cuff, waiting patiently like a respectable human being until she handed him his cup of tea. However, such a happy event was not to be, and John was deprived of the chance to revel in this simple yet sacred ritual between them when he heard Margaret sigh.

'There is no more tea,' she told her father without so much as batting an eyelash in John's direction to acknowledge the problem this posed to his thirst. 'I shall away and fetch more,' she decreed, and with that, she turned and left.

John's shoulders crumpled as he collapsed back into his chair. He was devastated to see her go. What if she did not return?

From John's glum position, he followed her every move, and his brow furrowed as he spied Margaret halting in the hallway. She dawdled there for a trice, unsure of herself, but then she put down the tray on a sideboard with one decisive motion before summarily scurrying upstairs. John lurched forward and nearly shouted out in churlish dissent. *No!* Where the blazes did she think she was going? The kitchen was downstairs, not up, so she had better not be planning to retreat to her bedroom and forsake him for the rest of the night. John sat there sweating, beads of anxiety trickling down his neck and wetting his shirt. Twiddling his thumbs at a dizzying speed, he could feel the dryness in his throat worsening as his dehydration increased, and he could sense his glands closing in as they thickened. For what must have been no more than a couple of minutes, minutes that were no longer or shorter than any other, since I have been expertly informed that such a thing is impossible, John was nothing more than a bag of nerves, engulfed by a fear that he had somehow insulted or upset Margaret, and that she was now making a point of refusing to see him. It may have been that he had offended her with the spoon. She could have seen it as an act of ridicule on his part, insinuating that it was her role to oblige him by tending to his every need, as if she were a maid and not a magnificent creature who was too good for this world. Nonetheless, hardly any time had passed before John heard the sound of somebody coming down the stairs, and there Margaret appeared again in the frame of the doorway. The master let out an audible sigh of reprieve, grateful beyond words that she was at least once again on the same floor as he. She now had something in her hands, a brown package wrapped with a blue ribbon. John wondered whether this might be the same parcel he had seen her wrestling with earlier when he stood outside, but he did not have time to inspect it further, because Margaret hastily tucked it under her elbow, collected up the tea tray, and then vanished down the next flight of stairs. John clicked his teeth. Well, it certainly looked as if she planned to come back, and that was better than nowt.

With his mind clear from the oppression of doubt, and now being content that his night was out of immediate danger from being entirely ruined, John returned his disgracefully erratic attention to his host. Poor Mr Hale had been speaking all this time, but about what, John could not even pretend to offer a plausible guess. Still, he was relieved to find that his tutor had not seemed to notice his discourtesy, and had himself filled in the gaps, most likely assuming his friend's lack of responsiveness was down to nothing more than his lethargy after weeks of travel. Be that as it may, despite John reproaching himself for his rudeness, and reminding himself that he should try harder to be more civilised, he found himself yet again breaking the rules of polite society when he recalled something Mr Hale had said earlier this evening.

Chapter Eight

The Definition of Friendship

'Mr Hale,' John interjected without so much as a tinge of tact. 'From whom did you hear that I was to be engaged?'

Mr Hale stopped and blinked at the question, unanticipated as it had been, particularly given that he had been talking about Aristotle, the name, Ann, never once leaving his lips. The ageing man took off his spectacles and scratched at the bridge of his nose as he trawled through his memory, unreliable archive that it was, full of dust and disorganised cataloguing.

'Why, from Mr Bell, I should think,' he said at last.

John blustered, and his eyes flashed with the incensed blaze of annoyance.

'*Of course*,' John retaliated with a terse hawk of his mouth, not the least bit surprised to ascertain the source of this vile rumour. Mr Bell had always been too wily for his own good, his proclivity for mockery and mischief well known in Milton. That is what inevitably happened when a man was indolent and did not have a trade to occupy his idle hands, he took up a sport, and that diversion was very often the hunting and killing of other men's good name for fun. After all, *those who are happy and successful themselves are too apt to make light of the misfortunes of others.*

Sensing his pupil's dissatisfaction, Mr Hale felt it only right to offer a further explanation. 'He told me that you were having a great deal to do with the Latimers of late, and that Miss Latimer had been spending a considerable amount of time at Marlborough House,' he began.

Grumbling under his breath, John was more aggravated than ever by this report, mainly because he could not argue with any of it. It was all true. For a start, he had been seeing a lot of Mr Latimer in recent months, more than he would have liked to, but that was all to do with business, seeing as he was a banker, and John a customer grappling with a state of increasingly concerning financial stability. As for Miss Latimer calling at his house, that was also correct, even if Mr Hale had been misled as to the reason for her attendance. Miss Latimer had never once been asked there as his guest, no, because she was always invited as his sister's friend, nothing more. If it were not impolite to say so, John would have noted how far from enjoying her presence, he found her artful sycophancy off-putting, and he did whatever he could to avoid her whenever she came by. For all that John was a man, and all men appreciate flattery, their insecure egos thriving on it, he was a shy person, and as such, he did not welcome toadyism in the way that others did. That is perhaps why he valued Margaret's company so highly. She just let him be himself, even if she disliked what *himself* signified, her lack of approbation a refreshing change.

'I believe he inferred that the young lady comes from a very good family and was considered an excellent match for a Thornton. You are, after all, both prominent families in Milton, or so I am told. Then what with the two of you being so well-suited, it was suggested that it would not be long until we were to hear the banns read in church,' Mr Hale concluded, his eyes wary as he cautiously watched the young man who sat before him hunched over in unease, afraid that he had overstepped the mark. He hoped that he had made it clear that this analysis was not his own, but Mr Bell's.

John nodded, even if his jaw was taught and his lips tight. 'He told you this?' he muttered. *'Just you?'* he checked, an impatient insistence to his last enquiry.

Mr Hale was yet again flummoxed by the irregularity of it all.

'Indeed. It was just the two of us, if I recall,' he confirmed, unsure of whom his friend thought might also have been privy to their conversation. The retired minister was a sheltered soul, he hardly saw anybody, so he was not one to impart gossip, either by nature, or by opportunity.

'And I hope you know that I would never breathe a word of your private affairs to anybody else, you have my solemn oath.'

The young man sniffed irritably in acknowledgement as his eyes fell upon the hearth, a mournful shadow dimming their keen clarity. This left Mr Hale feeling horribly uneasy, so he stood to stoke the fire while he deliberated over what to say next, the flames leaping higher at being so rudely poked-up, their red tongues lashing out at him with a crackling hiss.

'If I may, dear boy, I…'

'Go on,' John replied with a tone that resembled a snarl.

'I think you know that I am not the most observant of men,' his host confessed. 'It is all good and well when it comes to books, but when it comes to comprehending people, I fear I am ill-qualified.'

'As am I,' John countered, thinking on how badly he had misjudged his step when it came to Margaret.

He tried not to dwell on the mess he had made of things over the past year, a right pig's ear. It still struck him as profoundly ludicrous, that for such a careful and calculated sort of man, he had somehow allowed himself to make so many imprudent mistakes when it came to his first real experience of love. Falling for her as he did, John had known that Margaret did not harbour any degree of marked fondness for him when he had proposed, or at the very least, he had appreciated that she did not admire him in the way that a woman ought to admire a prospective husband. It was plain to him that she did not exalt him with the same passion that he cherished in his heart on her behalf, that would be an unattainable fantasy, even John had been able to see that through the mist of his infatuation.

And yet, when he thought about the way Margaret had rushed down from her sanctuary to aid him in his hour of need, a flicker of hope, obstinate blighter that it was, still burnt fiercely in his masculine breast.

There was no denying the way she had nobly shielded him from danger as she barricaded herself between him and the rioters. The way she had thrown her arms around his neck and clung to him for dear life, just so that he would not be harmed. As John closed his eyes and let the enamouring memory of her hands sliding along his cravat and grazing that slither of skin, that exposed flank of mortality that was not entombed in starched formality, flood him with a heady fever of desire, he dared to allow himself to hope, even for the briefest of moments, that she had at least cared for him in some small way. He still held onto this hope, implacably refusing to let it go, and so it would be, this pitiful, lonely man clutching onto this elusive glimmer of optimism throughout the chapters of his life, treasuring it until the bitter end.

While John was sinking into the depths of despair, Mr Hale was still grappling with his conscience, struggling to find the right words.

'But I...forgive me, I am not one to talk so unreservedly, nor, do I think, are you the sort of man to have his affairs discussed so openly,' Mr Hale stuttered, soldiering on with his clumsy speech, rousing John from his remote ruminations, somewhere far away, lost in the recesses of his troubled mind. 'I just wanted to say that I think I understand.'

John's expression must have been one of palpable confusion because Mr Hale proceeded to shake his head at his own incompetence before he resumed.

'I may not have known you long, John, but I hope I know you well enough that I may talk freely. And I believe that you have not been yourself of late. Your mood, it has been distracted, or rather, disillusioned. I thought it first to be the mill that was the cause of your unhappiness, – Mr Bell told me a little of your plight since the strike.'

What followed was a boisterous huff from John. Good grief! Was he all Mr Bell ever talked about?!

'However, I have given it a great deal of thought since your last visit, and after what Margaret said, (John jolted), I have reached the conclusion that it has nothing to do with that. I do not think you are perturbed by matters at the mill, or not as much as all that. You are a shrewd fellow, an industrious one, and you have survived challenges before,' Mr Hale contended, reddening at the forthright mention of John's past, not that the man minded, for he was not ashamed of it.

'To be sure, I think you shall take such strife in your stride and weather it better than just about any man I can think of.' Although Mr Hale did not let it show, he did allow himself a brief interim of personal reflection and self-pity at this point in his sermon. It grieved him to think that while John was a man of indisputable strength of conviction and courage, Mr Hale was sorry to say that he could not claim such a merit for himself.

'Thank you,' John allowed, still unsure of where all this was going.

'No,' Mr Hale continued, 'I think your problem is love.'

'*Love*?!' John blurted out. Oh, Lord! What *had* Margaret told her father? He had assumed that everything that had passed between them had remained just so, *between them*, but could it be that she had confessed all to one or both of her parents?

'Yes, love,' Mr Hale reiterated through a nervous cough. He had said it now, so there was no going back, no matter how uncomfortable he might feel.

'The thing is, I do know something of love, believe it or not. In truth, I loved my wife more than she ever knew,' he said sadly, the empty space in his heart where she had left a void crying like an abandoned babe as it wailed for her loss.

'I cannot talk of love with much eloquence. I could never write poems about it,' he admitted with a small chuckle, remembering the array of courtly verses the beautiful young lady had been sent by her numerous admirers, each of them making him feel hopeless and humdrum for being nothing more than a humble country clergyman who lacked their grand prospects and aspirations. Then again, she had chosen him. He could never fathom why, but Maria Beresford had chosen Richard Hale for her husband, and in turn, she had made him the happiest of men for twenty-six years.

'I could hardly speak of it, of this immense ache I felt for her, I was always too afraid, much to my eternal regret. But I know what love is, I have experienced it first-hand, and it is a fine thing. And all I shall say to you now is this...true love is rare, it is beautiful, and it is worth striving for. You are a good man, John. An honest man. A kind man. A principled man. Any woman would be lucky to share your name and share in your life. Miss Latimer could not ask for a better husband. Be brave, John,' he urged earnestly, '*be brave*, and she will love you for it.'

John gawped at him in silence. He was lost for words.

One half of him wanted to get up and hurl himself at Mr Hale, to fall to the ground and embrace him or shake his hand forcefully, the child locked away inside of him craving a father figure, and all the guidance and encouragement that brought. He had profoundly missed his own father over the past fourteen years, and to hear Mr Hale talk to him thus, by offering him advice in times of trouble and faith in his character, John could have wept. On the other hand, John's main concern was that Mr Hale should be immediately informed that while his sentiments were appreciated, his assumptions were false, fouler than the lies spat out by the Devil himself. It was imperative that Mr Hale knew that he did not, could not, ever want Miss Latimer to be his wife. While there was one person in the world whom John wished to know this unshakable fact above all else, it would not do for her father, the man he yearned to be his father-in-law, to think him capable of loving another, that the mill master's heart could be unfaithful to his beloved Margaret. Leaning forward, John was ready to denounce this claim, this allegation, once and for all. With a voice that was solemn and sober, he opened with,

'Mr Hale, I can assure you that you are gravely mistaken. It is not tru −'

However, John was cut short by his tutor, and not for the first time that night.

'Ah, here you are! We were starting to wonder where you had got to,' he declared as Margaret re-entered the room carrying a tray that boasted a fresh pot of tea and some scrumptious looking scones. John was conflicted. There was nothing he had wanted more than Margaret's speedy return, yet as absurdly contradictory as it was, he would have quite readily delayed her arrival by a mere minute, if only it meant he had been able to finish his sentence and tell Mr Hale that he was, and never would be, engaged to Miss Latimer. But no matter, it was perhaps best that Margaret was here, for now, because he would have the chance to apprise her of the fact too. Two birds with one stone, and all that. Nonetheless, when John went to open his mouth to utter his revelation, nothing came out, and he sat there like a codfish as Margaret poured him his tea and handed it over, a bemused look on her face to see the even more bemusing one overhauling his. He would have tried again, he really would, but Mr Hale, being more talkative than ever tonight, once again broke the interlude of silence.

'Now then, my good fellow, where was I?' he asked. 'Oh, yes, I wanted to know your thoughts on the subject.'

John's mien was as blank as an unblemished sheet of paper.

'I beg your pardon?' he mumbled, reluctant to make it known that he had not been paying the least bit of attention to what his tutor had been saying the whole evening.

'About Aristotle's writings on relations between men and women,' Mr Hale reminded him, and John noticed the way Margaret blinked in surprise at the vulgar phrasing used by her father. 'His question as to whether men and women can truly be friends, given their supposed fundamental differences.'

A meditative hush fell upon the room as all three people present contemplated this, each of them thinking their personal thoughts. Rotating his head just a fraction to the side to regard Margaret, John saw that she too was reflecting on the matter. She had given up her sewing, and with her teaspoon sluggishly looping round and round the rim of her cup, she scrutinised an unmarked spot upon the floor, her right eyebrow hitched as she considered her response.

'*Yes,*' John said at last, and he spied the way she twitched in her seat to hear him once again speak, her mind obviously elsewhere. With a spark of hope kindling within, he could tell that she was listening to him intently, so he vowed to himself not to waste this rare opportunity to say what he must.

'I think that men and women are not so different as people would have us suppose. It is true that they are anatomically distinct, and as such, there are things that one can do that the other cannot, such as the act of childbirth. And again, there are some things which one is better at doing than the other, such as carrying a heavy physical load. But these discrepancies are few and far between. I believe that there is more that makes us similar than dissimilar,' John advocated.

'Explain,' Mr Hale pressed, placing the tips of his fingers together in a pyramid as he lounged back in his chair and crooked one leg on top of the other, his joints grumbling in complaint.

The pupil paused as he considered where to begin. He was not a man for speeches, he never had been, always preferring instead to keep his opinions to himself. However, when it was something he was passionate about, John could match any orator who had ever lived.

'For a start, I do not think that women are lesser than men in any way. As a matter of fact, I think the opposite, and I often find myself wondering whether they are in fact far greater.' John then paused as he saw Margaret shift once again.

'High praise, indeed,' Mr Hale chortled with animation, nodding to his daughter in agreement, who, much to John's dissatisfaction, did not react to any of this, but that only incited him to continue.

'Women are depicted as weaker by nature, but I do not think a man can begin to imagine the strength it takes to bear and birth a child, and that is not counting providing that wean with love throughout its life. That takes a kind of determined willpower that is inspiring,' he insisted, thinking on the women he had seen in his mill who worked their fingers to the bone to provide for their families, all the while ignoring their aching backs as they carried a baby. He had seen more than one child born on his factory floor, and the screams of those mothers sent shivers through his very bones.

'And I do not believe for a minute that they are any less intelligent than men, despite what folk say. It is just that women are denied the chance to prove themselves as we can. If they were given equal opportunities to be educated and enter into the world of commerce, politics or the law, they would soon show us their worth, giving us a run for our money. And what is more, men are liable to be quick to anger, as well as being prone to arrogance and selfishness, a flaw which I firmly believe has led to many a tragedy, whether it be mindless wars that kill us dead abroad, or senseless laws that rob us of life at home. But women, while they can be as selfish as anyone, they know how to nurture, they spend their lives caring for others, and so, they are the ones best placed to decide what is to be done for the better, for the greater good.'

'And do you think women have a threshold?' Mr Hale questioned. 'Do you think there is a limit to how far they can be the equal of a man?'

As a man who had been outnumbered three to one by women for many years, Mr Hale did not hold these narrow-minded sentiments himself, for he knew how capable womenfolk were. But all the same, he wanted to hear what his pupil had to say, particularly since Margaret was present and would doubtless have a persuasive opinion of her own. Mr Hale was astonished that she had not spoken up more tonight. His daughter was never one to hold her tongue, that had always been the case for both of his spirited children, but then again, perhaps she was still feeling a trifle poorly, shame, when she had been in such jolly spirits just before John's arrival, watching and waiting for him at her window.

However, John was not quite done. 'We have a Queen, do we not, who sits on our throne? So if she can rule a nation, whilst also being a wife and mother, then why cannot all women rule their towns, their homes and their own lives?' John advocated, thinking of the most majestic woman he knew, and how he longed for her to be the supreme monarch of his small world. At this, he smiled to himself. He had spent his entire adult life cultivating autonomy, ensuring that he was the master of his own fate, and yet now, how he wished she would take the reins and allow him to rest awhile as she steered him in whatever direction she saw fit, because he trusted her compass implicitly, even more than he did his own.

'No, women are not lesser than men, they are greater, and because of this, I think not only are they entitled to be our friends, but that they should be encouraged to be so, not so much for their sakes, but for ours. For without women in the world, we are lost souls, adrift and deprived of their saving grace. I, for one, pray that I can one day find a good woman to be my friend, for I know that with her humanity and guidance, she could make me a better man,' he finished with a deep sigh.

'I am glad to hear it, Mr Thornton,' came an inconspicuous yet confident voice from across the room. 'Or else we could never hope to be friends.'

He sat up straight. She had spoken? Had she finally spoken to him?

John tried his best to tame his tone when he addressed her next. He was all too aware that the last time they had conversed in this room had been when he had insulted her and interrogated her trustworthiness, so it was essential that tonight, he did not sound anything but gentle and gentlemanly.

'And are we friends, Miss Hale?' he asked softly, his reverberation low, inviting Margaret to come out of her shell and open up to him.

Margaret wrinkled her nose at this, as if his suggestion had been illogical.

'That is not up to me,' she told him, returning her eyes to her cup, her pretty lips pursing indecisively.

John was unsure of what she meant, so he ventured a further question.

'So what, then, do you consider to be important qualities for someone who wishes to be your friend?'

She laughed. 'Why, friendship, of course,' she replied plainly. 'But I think my idea of friendship is perhaps very different to everybody else's,' she added thoughtfully.

'And what do you think it is, my dear?' her father prodded, and both John and Margaret startled with fright, since they had half forgotten that he was there at all.

'I know one thing, and that is that friendship is not always easy,' said Margaret straight away. 'Most people think that to be friends, two people must get along all the time. That they must always agree. That they must be similar in every way. But I do not think it so. Friendship can be hard to define, but it is definitely not all about smiles and laughter, nor is it grounded in the superficial art of congenial affability. Anybody can be friendly if they want to, that is not difficult. No, friendship, the word, the bond, it is about constancy and companionship.'

With a hand unconsciously rising to rub at the spot on her temple where she had been struck a few months before, Margaret distractedly murmured, 'It is about knowing that you have somebody who cares about you, who cares whether you are well or ill, happy or sad, alive or dead. They care that you are here, that you are in their life, that you exist at all,' she explained, her eyes glassy as she nibbled her lip.

'Sometimes people can grow angry with each other. Their feelings can become fragile. Hurtful things can be said. Mistakes can be made. But friendship, true friendship, sees beyond such petty things. It is stronger, resilient, and far more understanding than anything that might seek to break it. It recognises that people are human, and that they are imperfect, but it is about wanting to be there for another person, accepting them for who and what they are, with all their virtues and all their faults laid bare without criticism. For you see, without all this, they are not whole, they are not themselves, and how can we claim to love somebody if we do not accept all of them? It is about caring for a person unreservedly. It is about showing them respect, offering them encouragement, and minding how they feel and what they think. It is being there for them, regardless of what may happen, and showing them day in and day out that you are not indifferent to them, but that they matter to you, that you think of them.'

Letting her fingers skim her skirt, Margaret felt something in her pocket, and petting it, she discerned that it was a string of solitary wool, and this strange relic gave her the assurance she needed to say her piece.

'Friendship is showing somebody that you will always care about them...*always*.'

All this time, Margaret had been looking down, but as she finished, she peered up, and she was disconcerted to see both her father and Mr Thornton staring at her. While her father smiled and nodded, Mr Thornton did not move a muscle. His eyes, which she tried her best not to meet, lest she become lost in them, were unresponsive, his features and body language rigid, refusing to betray his thoughts. It was clear to her that he had not liked what she said, that he completely disagreed, and even though it hurt to think so, Margaret was still glad she had said what she did, and to him, of all people, and tonight, of all nights.

Blushing, Margaret picked up her sewing once more, and with a tremble to her voice, she concluded with:

'There, that is what friendship means...to me, anyway.'

Several minutes passed without another word being uttered, until, at last, the clock chimed the hour, and the three of them realised that it was getting frightfully late, that it was eleven o'clock, a mere hour until Christmas Day was upon them.

'I had better go,' John murmured half-heartedly, remembering that he had promised his mother and sister that he would see in the bells with them at midnight when they arrived back from their party. He had upset his mother enough by not staying home tonight, so returning now was the least he could do.

'Of course! Of course!' Mr Hale agreed, standing up and stretching out his arms, his old bones more than ready for a trip to Bedfordshire.

'Please, let me show you out,' he offered, aware that Dixon had been busy of late preparing for tomorrow's festivities, and so would greatly appreciate not being roused from her bed at this sleepy hour.

However, it was John who would have the final word, and on swiftly rising to his feet in one purposeful movement, he retorted with a brusque and commanding: '*No!*' before he decreed: 'Miss Hale will show me out.'

Chapter Nine

It Was...

It was true that Margaret had been discomposed by
Mr Thornton's request that she escort him out. It was
not so much that he had expected that she should do
so, because it was entirely natural for her to
accompany him to the door and politely see him on his
way. However, despite their well-practiced routine,
there were two things that did not rest easy with her
and left her feeling rather unsettled.

For one, she was surprised that he should want to be
in her company at all. He had been so cross and abrupt
with her in recent months, in the wake of his proposal,
or perhaps better termed as attempted proposal,
followed by his happening upon her at Outwood
Station in the arms of another man, and lastly, and
most severely, his hurtful and yet somewhat
understandable surge of censure when he had told
Margaret that he doubted her integrity. After all that
had passed between them, she could not divine why
Mr Thornton, this man who had revoked his interest in

her and severed his regard for her almost entirely, should ask her to remain in his presence, when surely, her presence was distasteful to him in every respect. Surely it would only serve to remind him of his humiliation at her unripe hand, and that was nothing compared to his lucky escape from being entangled with a woman who he now reputed to be lacking in credibility and moral fibre, two imperative pillars of character that he took most seriously indeed. Be that as it may, it was not only these facts that served to fluster her, no. The detail which threw Margaret the most, was the way he had said it.

Mr Thornton was, without question, a man who liked to assert his will. It was perhaps his rich and resonant voice that gave him that overbearing trait, or perhaps it was his physical stature, or perhaps it was his eyes and the way they pierced people and hooked them like a fish caught on a line, and no matter how frantically they squirmed under his incisive gaze, they were at his mercy until he chose to set them free. That was very possibly the real reason why Margaret had not looked at him as often as she might over the span of their attachment — *no*, that was too strong a word. Acquaintance? No, that was too weak, to be sure, too inaccurate. Association, then, that would have to do. At any rate, while he may have supposed it was down to apathy on her part, she could vouch that he had entirely the opposite effect on her. The unvarnished truth was that Margaret was afraid of becoming ensnared by Mr Thornton, the only problem being that it had already happened, and it was far too late to turn back, that particular train having left the station already. She did not know how, she did not know when, nor even why, but left it had, carrying her to strange new places, and if she were honest with herself, then she had no wish to look back, wishing instead to journey onwards in the adventure that is life, with him firmly and faithfully by her side.

However, there had been something different tonight, something altogether unforeseen in the many rehearsals she had played out in her mind of how tonight would go. Margaret had witnessed his domineering ways in practice, but never before had he asserted his inherent sense of authority in the Hale's home, otherwise opting to considerately leave his impression of officiousness behind at the mill gates. To be sure, Mr Thornton, while he had been gruff with her in the past, blinkered in his assertions of how he believed she should respond to certain situations in order to preserve and promote his own views, he had never once been dictatorial, showing that he respected Margaret's right to independence. Therefore, his insistent manner this Christmas Eve had unnerved her, for it was entirely out of character for the Mr Thornton she had come to know well, inherently so. Margaret had been tempted to say no, to defy him as a matter of both habit and principle, but alas, she found that she could not, so she had gone with him submissively.

Almost as soon as he had made his decree, John nodded to his host, and then began to walk out of the room and head towards the stairs without so much as glancing at the daughter. Margaret, as if under an inexplicable spell, rose to her feet too, trailing after him wordlessly, obediently, one might say. They continued down the stairs in silence, his head doggedly facing forward, naturally assuming that she was following his lead, even if he could not hear her graceful steps. When at last they reached the bottom of the stairs, John stopped as his attention was stolen by a twinkling of light off to his side. Moving in the direction of the parlour, like a moth gliding powerlessly towards a flame, he paused in the doorway, and he looked upon a most magical sight: the Christmas tree.

'Do you like it?' came a serene voice from behind him, an unmistakable hint of hope honeying it.

Now it was John's turn to be taken unawares. Only once before had he heard Margaret sound so meek and mild, and that had been on the day he had shouted at her most mercilessly, just a few paces away from where they stood now, the very spot sullied by his spite. With his heart twisting and tying itself in knots, John recalled the way his temper had broken under the strain of his onerous jealousy, and he had near enough accused her of being a wanton woman, as his slurs borne of nothing more than misery spewed forth from his mouth like devastating lava. That conversation still filled him with inconsolable remorse, keeping him awake many a night as he thought on how he would take it all back, if only he could. He had been a bully, and as for Margaret, she had been radiant in her punishment, more beautiful than he had ever seen her with her head hung low and her cheeks aflame under the fire of his scrutiny and scorn. It had commanded every last scrap of self-denial he had to tear his eyes away from her and continue up to his lesson, each step weighing him down like lead, his legs fighting to return to her so that he might hurl himself at her feet, cling to her skirts, and beg her forgiveness. He had a way of speaking to her curtly, it was a talent he possessed, roused by the unfamiliar passions she stoked within him.

John knew with a contemptuous spasm of contrition that he had been offhand in the way that he had demanded she show him to the door tonight. It had been rude, no way to speak to a genteel young woman, and while John knew that he could never manage Margaret like he managed his men, even if he wanted to, he had been guilty of discourtesy, and all because he *had* to see her, he *had* to be near her. *For all his pain, he longed to see the author of it. Although he hated Margaret at times, when he thought of that gentle familiar attitude and all the attendant circumstances, he had a restless desire to renew her picture in his mind - a longing for the very atmosphere she breathed. He was in the Charybdis of passion, and must perforce circle and circle ever nearer round the fatal centre.*

John simply *had* to know more about what Margaret meant when she had talked of friendship so vehemently. Even if he had wholeheartedly agreed with everything she had said on the subject, it had still been the strangest thing he had ever heard. Why had she said it? Why had she said it to him? And why had she said it to him tonight, of all nights? Casting his eyes down, John saw Margaret standing by his side, her hands folded across her midriff, her shoulder a fraction of an inch away from his upper arm, a section of bare skin teasing him with its creamy smoothness. He marvelled to think of how small she was. She was little, but *oh*, how she was fierce. Shakespeare must have somehow been imagining her when he had penned those immortal words. As Margaret stood beside him, enthralled by the tree, John took this opportunity to study her thoroughly. It occurred to him that he had never been afforded the chance to observe her from this intimate angle before. She had always stood before him, opposite him, ready to do battle, but now she was beside him, and there she had chosen to be, for now, at least. It made him think of marriage, the way that a man and wife stand side-by-side in church, and should they love each other truly, they will stand as one throughout the joys and woes of life. If he and she had wed, they would have stood like this often, he would make sure of it. They would talk, laugh, twitter in each other's ears, sharing secrets, smirks and smiles, her head on his shoulder, his arm around her waist. Measuring her with nothing more than his gaze, John decided that she was the ideal size for him. He had never thought this before about anybody, because for a start, he was too tall for everybody, but when it came to Margaret, his calculations told him that she could nestle snugly into his hold, rest her head on his chest, and he would place his chin on the crown of her hair, thus they would fit together perfectly, just like a jigsaw puzzle. Or better still, a made-to-measure part, such as for one of his machines, because just like his Spinning Jennies, John was beginning to realise that he could not function without this one crucial part that made him tick, that made him work, that kept him right, that made him whole, and that was Margaret. John felt a wrench to his heart to consider how else they would complement each other with absolute precision, stabilising their partner's virtues and weaknesses.

Spiritually? Intellectually? Sexually?

While there was no denying that he and Margaret were contradictory in almost every regard (and he did mean that, because they were forever contradicting each other), John was convinced that God had made them expressly for the sole purpose of loving each other, and so he had no doubt that while they may have been mismatched in terms of breeding, grace, appearance, and a hundred other trivial nothings, when it came to the heart, they were exactly the same.

As his contemplation swept over the contour of her cherubic face, John found himself transfixed by the wonder of her eyes as they stared ahead at the tree, sparkling like jewels, precious jewels that he longed to gaze at him with equal admiration and undivided affection. Lifting his head to follow her example, he sensed his heart stir to look upon such a heavenly sight. The tree stretched high, almost brushing the ceiling, its branches held out as it uncomplainingly took the weight of dozens of candles and baubles. The glow which exuded from it was hypnotic, the flames winking one after the other, sending rays of light dancing merrily around the room. John had no time for frivolous fancies, items that were ornamental opposed to useful, but for once he could say that he genuinely approved of this decorative shrine, and he was glad that he had acquired it for her as a Christmas present, a private and personal one from him to her.

'Aye,' he said at last, in answer to her question. 'I like it...very much so.' He could tell how much time Margaret must have spent festooning it, and it filled him with a rare sense of contentment to think that she had taken such care and pride in something he had given her.

Margaret had that way about her, a capacity for leaving everything she encountered that little bit more charming, an effortless ability that flowed from her feminine fingers. But it was more than that. While many women were artful and accomplished in turning plain or unappealing things into beautiful ones, Margaret did something even greater and harder to achieve; she made them homely. She smiled and looked up at him, her soft features as pretty as a picture, only, he was honoured to be so close to the real thing.

'Thank you,' Margaret whispered, her head tilting towards him, and for the briefest of moments, John could have sworn that she was readying to lay her head against him, but much to his disappointment, she suddenly halted and held it still.

John peered down the length of his arm to watch the way that her chestnut hair tickled the sleeve of his jacket, a few pins that contained her coiled pleats scraping along him. He was about to ask why she was appreciative, perhaps even to contradict her in some pointless way so that he might protect his pride, but he stopped himself. Such a line of enquiry would be senseless, because he knew exactly what she meant, and while he was used to being modest in his offerings, preferring to give discreetly without expecting thanks, he found that he craved her acknowledgement of his kindness, her recognition and gratitude for his thoughtfulness, so he held his tongue. Instead, he could have stood there with her for hours, lost in a trance of festive delights, but Margaret started to move away and wander towards the front door, the hem of her dress skimming his foot as she departed. John's heart sank to see her desert him. Ah, so she was thankful, but keen for him to go, all the same. Very well. He should not be surprised, he supposed.

No more was said for several minutes as Margaret fetched John his hat and coat. He could feel an icy wind sneaking in through an open window, and he shivered, intensely aware that he was about to be sent forth into the wilderness that was the unforgiving Milton winter without his gloves or a scarf to fortify him. As a Darkshire lad born and bred, John was used to adverse Decembers, but this had been the harshest he had ever known. It was almost as if the weather had sought to afflict him on purpose this year. After the strike, John had told himself that trade would soon pick up and that he and his fellow masters could dust themselves down and forget this whole sorry business. However, that had not been the case. It had proved to be a cool summer and autumn, and consequently, cotton clothes, which nobody wanted to wear, apparently, had seen a decrease in necessity, and as a tradesman, he relied on the fundamental concept of supply and demand to earn his bread and butter. Nevertheless, that was not the only reason John was reluctant to depart. Not only was it cold outside, but it was cosy right here, with her, the two of them standing close in the confined hallway, the heat of their bodies radiating into the restless air and warming them both as the vapour of their breaths drifted upwards in opaque clouds and mingled as one spectral dancer. It always happened this way. They both went about their days as people with normal temperatures, but then the moment they drew close, a wildfire ignited inside them, and before they knew it, they were scorched, hot and bothered by the knowledge that the one they yearned to hold close was near, the only problem being that they each wrongly assumed that they alone were stricken with this consciousness.

It was while John was thinking this, that he was distracted by an unfamiliar sensation, a pair of bewitching eyes watching him attentively. With an embarrassed scowl, he was irritated to realise that he had in fact finished adorning his clothes some time ago, and for the past minute and a half, he had been standing there like an imbecile, staring off into the distance with a vacant expression that made him appear a few grapes short of a basket of fruit. Good grief, she'd think him a halfwit. Trying to reclaim his flagging self-possession, John coughed self-importantly to clear the air.

'Miss Hale, I…I have been meaning to speak with you,' he commenced, frustrated to hear himself talk and to heed the detached tone that detracted from the purpose of his address.

'It was good to see you again tonight,' he said honestly, but with no small measure of hesitancy. He had to remind himself that this was the first occasion they had spoken alone following his speech denouncing his love for her, because every encounter since then had not only been infrequent, but overseen by others, so there was every possibility that Margaret had been holding back her anger towards him for speaking to her so offensively. John readied himself for an assault of her dander, or worse, the chill of her unreserved disinterest, but surprisingly, neither were bowled his way. She did not respond, and it appeared as if she had no intention to. Margaret merely lifted a finger and traced it along the wood of a nearby sideboard, as if inspecting it for dust, the lithe column skating along a horizontal path at its own leisurely pace. John had to look away. He could curse himself, but he felt like a boy of no more than fifteen, rather than a grown man of nearly thirty. Everything Margaret did had the power to enthral him. Every move of her body, no matter how innocent, fascinated him and provoked a primal hunger that lay deep beneath the surface, a door that he had never dared open, only now, he longed to fling it ajar and release all that repressed need upon her. He had lived in famine, and Margaret, she was his feast. Consequently, part of him was relieved that she was not entailed to endure such an indelicate onslaught of affection just to satisfy him, his want of her too intense for any one person to abide. Still, how John longed for Margaret to take that finger and run it along him, along the lines of his body so that she could learn him well and know him better, if only it would help her to discover the good in him.

'I was starting to believe that you were avoiding me,' he braved, and he saw the way Margaret's finger abruptly stopped, and she guardedly drew it back to her side, as if his words alone had wounded it, triggering him to wish he could snatch it up and kiss it fervently in hope of curing her ailment of angst inflicted by him and his careless mouth.

'I am sorry for it, for the way I spoke to you then,' he confessed lamely, realising that his regret was no good now. It did not absolve anything. It did not resolve anything. But at least he could try. 'I am more sorry than I can say, I just need you to know that.'

Nonetheless, much to his astonishment, Margaret's head jutted up, and her eyes met with his, searching him questioningly.

'You have no need to be sorry,' she told him directly, evidently amazed that he should imagine such a thing.

John too was caught off guard. But he would be careful, because the last time she had said that he did not need to feel the way he did, that is, that he had nothing to be grateful for, their conversation had taken an unpleasant and unfortunate turn, resulting in him picking a fight with the woman he loved during what should have been a romantic proposal. Passionate, it had been, that was true enough, but in all the wrong ways. Even so, on this occasion, she was wrong, he knew that was without question.

'Yes, I do,' he asserted flatly, accepting no argument this time.

'I was unforgivably discourteous. I should *never* have spoken to you like that, most especially in front of Mr Bell and your father, at a time when you presumably felt unable to defend yourself. I was out of sorts, so while I do not expect you to forgive my childish impertinence, please know that I regret it, and I promise never to speak to you like that again, I give you my solemn oath,' he swore, the fervour of his timbre intensifying as he went on, dissatisfied and discouraged by the fact that Margaret looked away from him and towards the floor, rendering it impossible for him to gaze into her eyes imploringly so that the sincerity of his heartfelt message could speak from his soul directly to hers. It was just like that night when she had chosen to look at her confounded sewing instead of him. If only she had looked up, even for a fraction of a second, then she would have known how sorry he was there and then. He waited for her response, and at length, Margaret nodded.

'I understand,' she appeased. 'You were unhappy. You were upset about the mill.'

John took a noticeable step back, and his neck creaked to the side with a swift force as he exhibited his confusion.

'*The mill?*' he repeated with incredulity. What the blazes did the mill have to do with any of it?

Shuffling from one foot to another, Margaret raised a hand and began to rub her arm, her shoulders huddled together as if she were a cornered animal. John could not understand it. She had never been shy around him before. He was so accustomed to her contempt, that he had no idea how to manage her distress. For so long, John had prayed that Margaret would bestow upon him one of her sweet smiles or cheerful laughs, but she had not, and now, as he stood before her tonight, he found that he would gladly go back to the days of her intolerable aversion, if only she would not look so sad. She had been different ever since his proposal, diffident, he would say. John told himself that it was perhaps to spare his pride further insult, only, that was more insulting by default. He could not stand this newfound timidness in her, it made him want to wrap her up in his arms and hold her close to dispel whatever fears or gloom beset her. He had to step back, again and again, distancing himself from her so that he could not do what he ached to, and that was to take Margaret by the shoulders and shake her, demanding that she look at him, and better yet, love him.

Picking nervously at her fingernails, Margaret conceded, 'Yes, my father and Mr Bell, they have explained that things have not been easy for you since the strike. They said that the mill is not doing as well as you would like.'

It was all true. Following the conversation with her father two weeks before, Margaret had sought Mr Bell out directly and pressed him for the facts, not relenting until he told her everything, even being called a bulldog in her own right, a veritable match for Thornton himself. With rising concern, she had listened painstakingly and noted Mr Bell's wary countenance, which contained a foreboding warning that if the mill did not recover within the succeeding months, it may have to close entirely. Margaret had been shocked, and after bluntly asking this and that to see what could be done, she had come to realise that Mr Thornton must have a merciless burden on his shoulders, so she was more than ready to forgive him his previous outburst.

Since then, it had absorbed her, consumed her, thinking about it long and hard, robbing her of concentration by day and sleep by night. Dixon had quite given up on her, muttering about how the young miss never did anything useful these days, she just sat and brooded. There had been one afternoon when Margaret had said she would peel the potatoes, only, an hour later, she noticed that she was still on the third one, a spud in one hand and a knife in the other, both suspended in mid-air. Her mind had ambled off to contemplate how Mr Thornton had been required to shoulder the weight of the world once before, and how unfair it would be if he were forced to bear such a millstone around his neck again now, after all he had achieved, after how hard he had worked to become the man he was today. It occurred to her that he would benefit from the steadfast support of somebody to console his concerns, a woman, perhaps, a wife, maybe, and as a tug of war between faith and fretfulness tussled within her, Margaret wondered who that lady would turn out to be. Well, she had wondered then, but now she knew, but she would not think on that, not just yet.

However, John, unaware of her compassionate interest in his predicament, thundered to hear this.

'*Good God*!' he raged, steam near enough whistling out of his ears. 'How does everybody know my own business better than I do?' he objected, thinking that he may as well hand in the towel, resign himself to his bed and his books, and let the likes of Mr Hale and Mr Bell manage his affairs for him. He was so inordinately riled, that John did not see the look of contrition written across her face.

'I am sorry,' she mumbled, conscious that she had overstepped the mark and intruded upon his privacy for a second time. Margaret was well aware that Mr

Thornton had already stipulated that she ought to mind her own business and stop interfering in his after she had sent Nicholas Higgins to Marlborough Mills to petition him for work, and here she was again, interfering where she was not welcome.

On hearing her voice falter, John's head whisked round to gauge her mood, and when he saw her lip wobbling, he could have punched himself squarely in the face for his unforgivable insensitivity. Here he was trying to apologise for his past tactlessness, only to go at it again with her, all hammer and tongs.

'No, no, I am the one to be sorry,' he sighed, raking his fingers through his hair in that way he always did when he was stressed. However, John did not do it for that reason alone, but to stop himself from taking her hand and clutching it tightly in the hopes of offering some inadequate reassurance that she was not at fault in the least.

'You are the one who has *nothing* to be sorry for.'

Peering up at him, Margaret's face suddenly took on a new bloom of hope, affecting the vessels of her blood to judder with an invigorated sense of life, flushing her cheeks with colour.

'Does that mean we can be friends, then?' she asked tentatively, an innocent childlike quality to her appeal.

Eyeing her for what felt like an age, John thought on this. His features were stern and set, making it impossible to read the conflicting thoughts that confounded him. Nevertheless, if one were to look closely at his eyes, those narrowed flints of steel, they would be able to see the torrent of indecision and insecurity that clashed behind those films of impassiveness.

'Is that what you want?' he countered, at last, unsure of his own answer.

The truth was that John did not know what to say to her in response. Did he want to be friends? Yes, he did. And then again, no, he most decidedly did not. The vulnerable part of him longed for her friendship, for her approval. Had he not just walked here this very night thinking that he had forfeited whatever was left of her good opinion? Yes, he had. It would therefore be the most unexpected Christmas gift in the world to find that Margaret Hale, the woman he had never before pleased, was willing to like him enough, respect him enough, to call him her friend. It would be better than nothing, it would be a lifeline, a chance for him to bask in her warmth and not be left to perish in the barren void of her disdain and disinterest. Yet, in contrast, it was not enough, and he knew it never could be. He grasped with a bittersweet sadness that he could never truly be satisfied with Margaret's friendship alone. His feelings for her were too manifest, too passionate, to allow mere friendliness to connect them slackly as they travelled through their days in parallel paths that never merged. They would forever be acquaintances, nothing more, nothing less, blandly passing the time of day, bearing witness to their disentangled lives that were not cemented by the assurance of requited love and longing. He would go about his business, building nothing more than an empty empire, and she, Margaret, she would meet someone, give her heart away, marry, have children, and possibly even be taken away from him to some happier place. Drowning in grief, John would be forced to watch helplessly from the side-lines, trudging a solitary road that would never lead to her. No, it would not do. He yearned for a stronger bond, a more sacred tie that would bind them as one for life throughout thick and thin. John wanted to tell her that her friendship was worthless to him, because, in the end, it would suffocate him, her niceness, her politeness, her insufferable indifference, and over time, the desperation he felt to hold her, kiss her, know her, it would become too much, and he would shatter from the pressure of it all simmering inside him, unable to find release in the form of calling her and making her his wife.

As he wallowed in these dark thoughts, John's eyes were bowed to the ground, but his head nudged upwards as he heard her say something, the earnestness in her voice endearing enough to break the desolate spell that he had cast upon himself and spat on him from above like a rain cloud, soaking his soul and saturating it with melancholy, disintegrating its stores of hope until they washed away into the gutters of his self-doubt, drains that ran deeper than Hell.

'I have something for you,' Margaret announced, and turning away, she bent down to retrieve something from a cupboard compartment in the sideboard.

John watched with intrigue as she crouched and rummaged around, her tongue sticking out of her mouth slightly at an angle as she did so, a comical spectacle that would have made him laugh if he were not feeling so tired and tense. After a few fumbling moments, she pulled out a brown package tied with a blue ribbon, a self-satisfied look on her face. His eyebrows then rose voluntarily to scuff his temple, articulating his unmistakable surprise. He had completely forgotten about the parcel that Margaret had fetched earlier and carried downstairs along with the tea tray. It was remarkable to recall how engrossed he had been by this mystery not half an hour before, only now, John was more gripped by an acquisitive curiosity than he could say to hear that it had something to do with him. Returning to hover before him, Margaret held the parcel possessively in her hands. She stared at it for a while, as if inspecting it, or perhaps deciding whether she did indeed wish to part with it after all, the contents being her primary and most private companion for two weeks, and she had grown fond of it in the interlude. After a fleeting lull of hesitation, she nodded to brace herself, then lifting her eyes to him, she also lifted the parcel, indicating that he should take it. Reaching out, John did as he was bidden, aware that as he clasped it, his fingertips bumped hers, and the pair of them convulsed, waves of static shock shooting throughout them. John did not know whether he was supposed to open it now or wait, but for a man who knew all about staying power, he found that he was as impatient as a child on Christmas Eve. Gripping the paper, John began to rip at it, far more greedily than gentlemanly, until, finally, the wrappings fell away, and he was left standing with something entirely unanticipated in his hands.

It was blue. It was soft. It was beautiful.

It was a scarf.

Chapter Ten

Friends, Indeed!

Holding it up to the light, John stared at the scarf, his eyes attentive as he studied it avidly, and in his rapt silence, he did not notice the way Margaret nibbled her bottom lip nervously, struggling to assess his reticent reaction, unforthcoming as it was.

'It is not much, I know,' she acknowledged, suddenly feeling tremendously silly for giving him something so pitiful as her unexceptional efforts when he could have bought a scarf that was much more splendid and fitting for a gentleman of his standing, 'but —'

'You made this?' John interrupted. '*For me*?'

Margaret sniffed self-consciously as she smoothed down the creases in her skirt, wondering whether her letter had arrived by now to thank Dolores for the material that had been used to make the frock, her new sister-in-law having sent the reams of cherry-hue silk and satin to her, all the way from Spain.

'Yes,' she admitted, as quiet as a mouse, unsure of whether he would approve or disapprove of this fact.

Now that she paused to reflect on it, Margaret realised how ridiculous it all was. How could she explain herself? It was not every day that an unmarried woman gave an unmarried man a present, particularly when they were not related. Besides, he had given her a tree, a glorious symbol of Christmastime, and she had returned Mr Thornton's generosity by favouring him with nothing more than a meagre scarf that had more slip-ups to recommend it than merit.

Nevertheless, John's appraisal was entirely different. Resuming his assessment of the scarf, he turned it over in his hands to inspect it more closely. It was perfect in its imperfection. It was lengthy and thick, but not extravagant in either way, and the yarn was robust yet delicate, promising to wrap his neck in woollen warmth. There were tiny holes here and there marked by frogging, nothing really, but it was charming to think, rendering it seamless to his eye, because it told him that Margaret, despite her flawlessness, could make mistakes. The thought that she had made this with evident care caused his heart to gallop in his chest, and while his former self would have doubted that true forethought had been knitted into its folds, loop by loop, there was a demonstration of dedication to every purl. But there was one detail which interested him the most.

'And the colour?' he enquired, his eyes darting up to study her own before swooping back down, secretly trying to compare and contrast the two, his report telling him that they were an exact match.

Suddenly feeling terribly abashed under the weight of his scrutiny, Margaret ducked her head and examined the rug beneath her feet.

'Dixon said it is your favourite, or so she heard you say, but I may have got that wrong. If it is not to your liking, then you need not wear it,' she allowed, disappointed by his dislike of it. Margaret knew it was not an exceptional scarf, but she had at least thought it would meet with his satisfaction and be adequate to complement his moderate tastes. If she had known Mr Thornton would be this particular about it as he near enough nit-picked every stitch away, then she would not have taken the trouble. Huffing to herself, Margaret moved around him, her elbow knocking his with tormenting friction, and she went to open the door so that this awkward interview might promptly come to an end, and she could retire to her bed to try and forget it all in what would doubtless be a fitful sleep. But before she had a chance to see her plan through, Margaret paused, and spinning round, she leaned against the wood, trapping him inside. Fixing him with a determined stare that both excited and unnerved him, Margaret ventured to ask: 'May I say something?'

John's expression was a curious one, coming across as a bewildered demeanour that fell somewhere between interest, puzzlement and amusement, unsure of which emotion to settle on.

'You have never sought my approval before, Miss Hale, so I see no need for you to seek it now,' he replied, his tenor a composite of sincerity and tongue-in-cheek playfulness, his eyes flashing with the flirtation of it all. Nevertheless, Margaret, dear girl, in her innocent naivety, did not understand his jest, and took his comment as one of ridicule for her impertinent ways. Nonetheless, she would not be daunted, so with a glowering pout, she continued.

'I know that a great deal has passed between us,' she started, her eyes naturally wishing to look away and escape him in demure mortification, but she refused to let them do so, instead, she directed them to stare at a lonely bristle about half an inch away from his right sideburn that he must have missed when shaving, settling upon this as her intractable focal point.

'As I say, a great deal has transpired, a great deal that is a pity, but I want for all that to stop. I know that it has all been my fault,' Margaret then proclaimed, and John's head tilted to the side as he regarded her with intrigued perplexity, and it took every ounce of self-discipline she had not to reach out and stroke his stubbled cheek.

'You have been nothing but generous to my family. You were patient with me while I attempted and often failed to find my way here, and I have repaid you with prejudice and false accusations against your character, none of which you deserved, not then, and not now. I cannot take it back,' she said unhappily, clearly upset by the obstinate fact, 'although I wish with all my heart that I could. But I promise that I shall try and be better, that is, if you will have me, for your friend.'

Listening to this, John was astounded, unable to respond. He had come here tonight with the intention of apologising to *her*, not for it to be the other way round. He knew Margaret to be a munificent sort of woman, but one who was resolute in all that she said and did, so once she had said or did what she said or did, then she would not unsay or undo it. Therefore, while her cruel retorts on the day of his failed proposal still echoed in his ears, he had never once dared to hope that she might regret a single word of her fatal rebuttal to his declaration, short as it had been. Lost in a myriad of jumbled thoughts, he was still trying to work out what he thought to all this when she announced: 'And there is something else.'

The mill master's eyes slanted, unable to deduce what else there could possibly be.

'Go on,' he incited, there being more suspicion than willingness to his invitation.

Turning away, and taking his unruly heart as she went, Margaret hid herself as she reached into the pocket of her dress to liberate something, the single strand of wool from earlier falling out as she did. This time, when she returned to face him, she held an artefact that was much smaller and less distinguishable close to her stomach, covering it charily with her palms and firmly scrunched fingers. Taking a few deep breaths, she finally let her hands fall, and there, she revealed two gloves, a pair: both long, both black, both leather, both his. John examined them carefully in the frail light of the hallway, his preoccupied gaze roaming across the familiar skin of the hide with all its well-worn tarnishes of time and labour. His mind knew fine well what they were and whom they belonged to, but his heart, his wounded heart, it could not begin to understand why *she* should have them, nor why she was holding onto them so compellingly, almost as if her fiercely protective grip spoke of a special bond between her and these simple gloves, as if she were saying goodbye to a friend, knowing that duty dictated that she must part with them forever. Trembling, Margaret squeezed them tight once more, and then gradually, she raised them up to him and placed them on top of his scarf, letting them go, taking her hands away with a slow and sad wilting, the act more symbolic than he would ever know.

'I wish you well, Mr Thornton,' she said with a quivering whisper.

Taking a deep, steadying breath, Margaret prepared herself to say what she knew she must, what she had been building herself up to say for the past three hours, ever since she had heard her father welcome Mr Thornton into their home tonight. During those minutes, she had overheard something that she had long suspected, but until now, had refused to believe was true.

'Miss Latimer is a fine lady, in every sense of the word, and she will make you a fine wife, finer than I ever could,' said Margaret, disparaging herself. 'She is handsome. She is accomplished. She is obedient. And she knows the ways of Milton. She will never disappoint or disgrace you by being opinionated in public and headstrong in private. I only hope that when you are wed, you shall not forget us,' she requested with a forlorn lilt to her usually clear-cut voice.

'Father so enjoys your visits, and I do too, because despite my absence of late, I have missed you,' she admitted, a blush inflaming her cheeks like splashes of scarlet paint.

'So please, do not forget us completely, although I am sure you will be busy. You will have a new wife, and with her, a new family that will surely come, they being your priority now, I am certain of it. Some men would not pay such responsibilities much notice, but not you, Mr Thornton, *no*, you shall dedicate yourself to their happiness every moment you are awake, I know it,' Margaret added with a fond smile, thinking how there could be no finer husband or father than he.

'Perhaps next year we will see you here again, and we shall be able to welcome Mrs John Thornton to our humble abode. And possibly even your baby together — *oh*!' Margaret exclaimed, her body shuddering at the thought of it, but she quickly sniffled and smiled in a way that was too merry to be genuine as she tried to mask her pain.

'A baby is just what this house needs,' she went on, elevating her watery eyes upwards as she peered at the upper floors, rooms that would remain as barren from the seed of a child as her womb was doomed to be.

'I am sure yours will be quite lovely,' she affixed, her gaze flitting up and down him surreptitiously, aware that it was perhaps improper to point out such a thing, her angst-ridden mind daring to imagine it, tormenting her with dreamy visions of a handsome baby boy with black hair and blue eyes.

'So, you see...I wish you well, Mr Thornton, from the bottom of my heart, I wish you well,...*as my friend*,' Margaret concluded, finishing what had been the most distressing homily of her whole life, but one which she needed to say, needed to let drain from her, not only for his sake, but her own, all so that she might be bled of the poison of repentance that had infected her for too long. What followed was an intermission of silence, in which neither of them said a word, their heartbeats the only sound that could be heard, loud as they were, hammering amidst the hush that deafened the space between them.

Then, all of a sudden, the air whipped up into a frenzy as John hissed: '*Friends, indeed!*'

She flinched with fright, and Margaret's elegiac eyes climbed the length of him to search his own so that she might determine whether she had misinterpreted his harsh manner, and find only tenderness there, but alas, they were alight with anger, his quaking body rigid with rage.

'We are not friends!' he condemned with a scoff. It was frightening, really, he did not shout, but Margaret rather wished he would, because there was something altogether eerie about the way he spoke. It was restrained, yet not subdued or dulled, but in opposition, it was more potent, more powerful, more passionate than ever.

'We have *never* been friends, and we *never* can be,' he informed her, his eyes burning fiercely.

'I do not understand!' she cried. Margaret had no notion of what she could possibly have said to incense him so. She knew that she had been guilty of tossing thoughtless words his way in the past, but tonight, she had tried, she had truly tried to be good, to be gentle, to be generous in all she said, desperate not to hurt Mr Thornton further.

Striding towards her, swaggering with the strength of his emotions, John leaned in closer, eclipsing Margaret with his towering shadow as he refused to let her go without learning the uncompromising truth.

'I shall tell you *exactly* what you are to me, Miss Hale –'

But he did not have the chance to say what he wanted, his testimony dying on his lips as Margaret flew away from him, retreating backwards with staggering steps and knocking into the sideboard, her eyes wide and wild with alarm.

'*No!*' she resisted. 'Pray, do not say another word,' she begged, reminding him with a brutal stab to his raw heart of that day, not so long ago, when she had forbidden him to continue. 'Think very carefully before you speak, Mr Thornton, because once you do, you cannot take any of it back, and I should hate for you to regret its saying, and I, its hearing.' She wanted to offer him her unconditional support, she did, but she was not yet ready to hear how inconsequential she was to him. Margaret knew that she was being a coward, but he was asking too much, it was simply too much to bear on a night that ought to be pregnant with hope.

Again, there was silence, the two of them panting as they stared at each other in the darkness, the flickering lamps casting disturbed shadows upon their faces, illuminating their despair and snatching it away like the blackened claw of grief. Finally, John took a step back, defeated once and for all in his pursuit of love, and then he nodded solemnly.

'Very well,' he assented coldly, 'as you command, *my lady,*' he said with a derisive bow of his head.

Picking up his hat, gloves and scarf, John readied to leave, but as he did, he looked up and spied a single stem of mistletoe peeking out and hanging down amongst a mass of ivy. Glaring at it, he reached up, and with one swift swoop of his hand, he snatched it down, crunching it in his grasp, his contorted face hiding the affliction he felt as the needles speared his skin. Earlier this evening, he had been working himself up to believe that he could accept the idea of Margaret being with somebody else, so long as she was happy and secure in life, but not now. He had changed his mind. A venal and cynical resentment had taken hold of him, and all John knew was that if Margaret did not love him, then he would be damned if he would sit back and watch her love another. *He knew how she would love. He had not loved her without gaining that instinctive knowledge of what capabilities were in her. Her soul would walk in glorious sunlight if any man was worthy, by his power of loving, to win back her love.*

Swerving on his heels, John heaved open the door, and marched out into the wintry night, turning his back on this house and all the hopes it had hitherto contained, vowing never to return. Margaret watched in dismayed stillness as he walked away, his muddy footsteps trodden into the snow that had been formerly swathed in white, untouched in its virginity, echoing the way she had trampled over his heart before, that fragile organ of purity never to be unaffected again, forever to be imprinted with the mark of love. She was stunned, and it was not until the belligerent wind that billowed in through the open door nipped at her cheeks that she realised that they were stinging with water from the salty river that leaked in unseemly gushes from her eyes. Rousing herself and regaining her wits, Margaret wiped away her tears, and she sprang forth, running after his vanishing shadow. As she twisted her head, she searched the street frantically, her vision impaired by the snowflakes that fell in clusters that were somehow mutually fluffy and dense. She could not see, so shielding her eyes with her arm, Margaret squinted, and then, much to her relief, she saw Mr Thornton, halfway down the road, not far from the corner that would steal him away from view. Making sure to close the door behind her so that Dixon and her father would not be alerted to her absence, Margaret rushed down the steps and hurried to catch up with him, her feet promptly turning wet and miserably cold as she struggled to sprint in her silken house shoes that were made for comfort, not a chase.

'Wait!' she called out after his retreating form. 'Mr Thornton, wait, *please*!'

Chapter Eleven

Will You Not Have Me?

Margaret was running as quickly as she could, but it was tricky as she stumbled in the thick snow that hindered her legs from making significant strides, her skirts weighing her down and her toes being nipped at by the frost that nibbled at them like tiny white mice.

'Stop!' she called out urgently, but he did not listen.

'Wait, stop, I cannot — *oh, dear,* — I cannot run!' she pleaded, faltering and falling forwards as she tumbled downwards, her gloveless hands diving into a glittering mound of snow and stinging. When he still did not halt, despite surely being able to hear her distress, Margaret found that her sense of charity had reached its breaking point, and her patience ran out.

'Mr Thornton, you will stop at once!' Margaret shouted, coming to a standstill and refusing to make a fool of herself by chasing after him for a second longer, absurdly tracking him through the streets of Milton in the middle of the night.

'I demand it!' she insisted.

It was true that Margaret was ready to excuse Mr Thornton's volatile moods of late, the poor man had a great deal to contend with, and therefore, she appreciated that she should tread gently where his feelings were concerned. Even so, there was no way she was going to tolerate his fits of temper if they were not explained, tantrums that were not only as contradictory as day and night, but came and went just as rapidly. Shovelling her foot into the snow, Margaret kicked it hard, and a colossal heap of the stuff went flying into the air in a spray of powder-like frost and pummelled Mr Thornton on the back with a thump. Her ploy worked, because he came to an immediate stop, even if he remained taut with anger, his back still turned away from her in unwavering resentment.

Oh! Oh, my! She was quite impressed with herself for that.

Margaret puffed with frustration as she marched towards him like a man, *sorry*, *woman*, on a mission.

'That is better,' she muttered, wiping her hair away from her face, trying not to think what a dreadful fright she must look after this short yet stressful ordeal.

Finally, Margaret managed to catch up with him, her legs not nearly as long as his, but she soon preceded Mr Thornton, coming to stand a few yards in front of the mill master who just stood there, rooted to the spot, resembling a black statue that starkly contrasted with the white of his surroundings. She saw at once the conflict in his face. His nostrils were flared, his chin was jutted, his jaw was tight, but even if his eyes were seething with something akin to wounded pride, they scanned her with blatant concern when he caught sight of her, evidently troubled that she should be outside without so much as a stitch of clothing other than her negligibly thin dress that was made for an evening tucked up safe indoors by a roaring fire.

John was about to insist that Margaret go back inside, to take her by the wrist and drag her there, or better yet, to collect her up in his arms as if she weighed no more than the parcel she had just given him and carry her, ignoring her shouts of protest and offended slaps. In the end, he gave in, accepting that there was no way he could tell her what to do, not when she was clearly indignant already, so removing his coat, he stripped down to his waistcoat and shirt, and moved to place the heavy garment over her shoulders, carefully pulling the lapels so that it covered her as fully as possible. Margaret trembled under his unexpected gentleness, the brush of his fingers disturbing the fine hairs on the back of her neck, stirring her senses to the tenderness of his touch, but she did not mind it, not at all. She could have objected, insisting that it was his and that she could manage perfectly well without his chivalrous assistance, but alas, her body was numb from the cold, save for the jabs of icy discomfort that pricked at her nerves, so she let him have his way, just this once. With a winded breath that blew into the air like an obscure cloud and scattered, she said what she knew she must.

'Mr Thornton, I cannot think what I have said tonight that has angered you so, but I am sorry for it, truly I am. I will listen to whatever it is you have to say and accept it. I will not stop you this time,' she pledged, reminding him not so subtly of a day when she had prevented him from speaking what he wished, sentencing him to silence, ordering him to walk away with the secrets of his heart still unburdened, rendering it more burdened than ever, all thanks to her disservice.

'You shall be free to tell me all that you will, all that is in your heart, and I shall not shrink from it, you have my word.'

John laughed, a short, sarcastic laugh, and his head fell back as he gazed at the moon that was full and bright, his mood difficult to infer as he contemplated how small and insignificant he was compared to the immeasurable universe that stretched above him. These constellations had surely witnessed many a scene as they lay belly-down upon their canopy of black swirls. Some dramas would have been wretched, some cheerful, some with happy endings, some with tragic final curtains, and he wondered what the stars made of him tonight, whether they were mocking him for his foolishness, or whether they wished upon themselves that his humble hopes would defy all impediments and prevail.

'Why did you make me this scarf?' he asked at length, his attention once more returning to her, not that it had ever truly been elsewhere, his eyes penetrating as they fell upon her sad face, casting a spell and remanding Margaret so that she might answer his all-important question.

At first, Margaret was distracted. She was hurt that he did not put on her scarf, instead allowing the frost to settle on his neck and melt into pools of water that drenched the collar of his shirt. It made her cross to think that Mr Thornton would rather be ill than wear her gift, but she had wounded him tonight, although she did not know how, so Margaret forgave his refusal to accept her offering, given that she too had once refused him, and much more harshly. She still believed that he did not like it, but whether he was slighted by the modesty of its creation, or the identity of its creator, she was yet to find out. Shrugging her shoulders, and feeling at an utter loss for how to rationalise the situation, Margaret did not know what to say.

'Because I could not bear for you to be cold!' she answered simply, because it was perfectly true. She had hated the thought of him walking about town, always busy, always diligent, always unselfish in his pursuit of doing right by others, never once thinking of himself and caring for his own needs. Mr Thornton may have been a strong man, but even strong men need shelter from the bitterness of this world.

'And because I was sorry. I wanted to offer you an olive branch, and I have nothing else to give,' she professed, holding out her empty hands to express her hopelessness. Margaret understood that she had nothing Mr Thornton needed, nothing he wanted. No money to relieve his plight. No skills to appease his labour. No words of certainty in the future to both confront his fears and comfort his hopes. However, there was one thing Margaret could give him, no matter how worthless it might be, and that was her unconditional friendship.

'And from what little I know, friendship is about giving, not what you get back in compensation or as a reward. It gives honestly and openly without expectation. It is not selfish. It is not grasping. It keeps no records of what is owed or spent, of what has been done right and what has been done wrong. It is malleable in times of turmoil, and it is persevering in its loyalty, recognising that people are flawed but still worthy of human compassion and comfort. It just wants to bestow whatever little it has, and it does so freely and gladly besides. And I made it for you because I wanted you to know how I feel about you.'

John's breathing was now so fitful, that he could scarcely draw breath.

'And how do you feel? *About me*?' he whispered, his voice deliriously uneven as he took a cautious step towards her.

Margaret sniffed as her nose began to snivel, and she folded her arms over her midriff to shelter them.

'I care about *you*,' she confessed, a hand breaking free from its huddled hold to sweep towards him, no longer ashamed of admitting it.

'You have come to mean so very much to me. I cannot pretend to understand it all. In fact, I can barely understand it *at all*, try as I might. I can hardly recollect how, when or why you took up such a special place in my heart, but you have. Indeed, there is so much of you there, that I wonder if there is any of myself left,' she laughed, a hand kneading the top of her breast where her awakened heart beat fiercely. She thought of him so often these days, that Margaret half wondered whether, after all, she was him, or he was her, it was all so strange.

'You have embedded yourself there, I believe, never to be removed, and do you know what, Mr Thornton? I am glad of it!' she avowed, stepping towards him purposefully, showing him that she would no longer hide away from him.

'It both scares me and fills me with such security to know that I will always have you here, close to me, no matter how far away you may be in every other respect.'

Margaret could not help but reproach herself for her past errors, ones that seemed like a lifetime ago, when, in fact, it had merely been a year since their paths had crossed, and in doing so, their divergent lives had connected, their dissimilar worlds collided, and their destined souls correlated. She wondered how it would have been if they had never met. Could it be that these two people, these two twins of heart, could have gone through life existing without the knowledge of the other? No, she thought not, for that would be impossible, and they would always have felt like a piece of them was missing, a vital portion of themselves that they must find, lest they die detached, diminished and in despair.

Nevertheless, it was too late. Her heedlessness had erected an unforgiving wall between them, never to be dismantled, she feared. They would never be truly close in any way, other than this, other than now, in this very moment. He would continue to think of her with derision, his enmity slowly giving way to detachment over time. They would scarcely see each other when he married, his time rightly taken up with his new and growing family. And while Mr Thornton did not live far away at present, one day, Margaret would be sent away from him permanently, she knew it would be so. When her father died, hopefully many years from now, she would be packed up and packed off like a bequest and sent to live with Fred or Edith, her family obliged to take care of their spinster relative. After that, she would never see him again, her memory the only way of recalling his face.

Because of this impending conclusion, Margaret could not help but stare at him. She had usually shied away from his discerning gaze in the past, a look that revealed his feral feelings for her, but not tonight. Tonight she would look at him boldly and unblinkingly, memorising every inch of that face that characterised to her mind the very definition of handsomeness and honour.

John was unsettled by her stare, but he matched it, negating to look away as he stepped closer, dangerously nearer, daring to disturb the nest of their confessions.

'I was wrong about you. I see that now,' she admitted unreservedly, her eyes mapping his features, thrilling him as she did, as if she had reached up and touched him with her own dear hands.

'I judged you harshly in my naivety. I knew nothing of Milton, or masters, or men, and so I responded how I thought best, based on the sheltered little that I knew, or thought I knew in my arrogant youth. But I have come to learn that I was gravely mistaken in my assumptions, and yet while my immaturity may be pardoned, I will always be ashamed of my atrocious pride, for which I have no excuse, and now must pay the price. Still, while I can be quick to anger, and am known to be, at times, critical, one of my other faults is that I am stubborn,' she said zealously, her eyes animated, 'and I vow to stubbornly be your friend, every day for the rest of my life, John Thornton, regardless of whether you want me as your friend.'

John sighed, the noise that emitted from him boisterous and aggrieved, as if she had driven a knife straight through his heart.

'Stop saying that!' he censured, the sound cracking like thunder in the frigid sky.

She was dismayed. Margaret wobbled on the spot, mirroring the unpredictable shifting of his own form as he spun away from her and combed his fingers through his hair in agitation. Margaret was extremely confused. She had never been particularly diplomatic with her words, but at least she tended to know when she was inflicting pain, whether that be intentional or incidental, and she had tried hard, so very hard, to be kind to him tonight, so why was he so unhappy?

'Saying what?' she asked, inept to guess.

'*Friend*!' he snapped, spitting it back at her through gritted teeth. 'That odious word. I hate it! I do not wish for us to be friends!' John decreed, shaking his head adamantly.

He was so incensed, that he did not see the little colour that was left in Margaret's cheeks pale as she listened to him, her face aghast, as if he had just struck her, not that he could ever do such a thing.

'Then what *do* you want?' she beseeched, at a loss to know what else she could give him. Was it nothing? Was that the answer? Did he want nothing from her? Nothing with her? Nothing to do with her? Oh! She prayed not, because that would be too much to ask, too much to give.

'I am not marrying Ann Latimer.'

The fact spilled from his mouth like a blundering splutter, and Margaret froze, unable, although not unwilling, to believe her own ears.

'Why not?!' she interrogated, rather rudely, because Margaret was astounded by this revelation.

'She is right for you; you are right for each other. I am sure she will be honoured to be your wi −'

John groaned loudly. 'Heaven help me!' he cursed, sick and tired of her ingenuousness. 'Because I love *you*, Margaret!' he let slip, gesturing towards her.

It was almost as if the whole world went quiet and the two of them were all that were left awake. Margaret's mouth fell open and hung quivering in bewilderment.

'*What did you say?*' she breathed.

'You heard me. *I — love — you*,' John repeated, stalking towards her, his steps so calculated that it was almost terrifying, almost as if he were daring her to run from him, testing her against the strength of his ardour, because if she could not bear the intensity of it now, God help her if and when he unleashed the full force of his passion upon her. But Margaret did not budge, she held her ground valiantly, *and God!* – how he loved her for it.

'*Why?*' she had to know.

Moving so close to her that their noses almost touched, John came to stand before Margaret, his gaze holding her in place, the heat of his breath falling upon her face and warming her through and through. He thought about how he had impulsively tried to be near her on the day of his proposal, when he had rounded the table to come to her, but she had evaded him and withdrawn, so it inspired him more than he could describe to find that she did not flee now.

'You say you are stubborn? Well, so am I! I am as stubborn as stubborn gets, it is what got me this far in life. And I have never, *never*, been as stubborn about anything as I am about loving you. You ask me why I love you, and the answer is God alone knows. You are infuriating, Margaret, you are insufferable. You are impossibly perfect, despite being a nightmare of a woman who haunts my every waking and sleeping moment,' he said tersely, tortured by his longing for her.

'I cannot escape you, I cannot get over you, struggle in torment as I might. You give me no peace, yet I know that you alone can bring me it. You drive me mad, but the Devil take me, I am yours, and always will be. You are stamped on my soul, and I am no longer whole without you. Everything I do, everything I think, and feel, and am, they are all governed by my love for you, my one defining wish being to make you happy and to selfishly ask that you make me happy in return. You see, you are too good, dear heart, you say that friendship and love are noble things, and I am sure you are right, they are righteous in their pure form, but I am too hungry a creature for such decency, and I crave your undivided affection to be the recompense for my faithful and fond devotion for all our days. I could no more stop loving you than I could stop breathing, for without my hope of you, I would die.'

John then retreated ever so slightly to give her room to breathe, the space that decorum dictated he must. Lifting her scarf and holding it firm in the narrow disparity between them, so close that the wool stroked both his cheek and hers, he insisted once more upon knowing the truth behind her unexpected gift.

'So I ask you again, Margaret, why did you make me this scarf?'

Nodding with the confidence of her unshakable conviction, Margaret took a step towards him, closing the gap between them, her chest just touching his and no more, the precise amount too small to measure, the sensation igniting irrepressible embers to burn in their breasts.

'Because I love you,' she told him fearlessly, 'and because I have nothing else to give you to show you how I feel.'

John panted. 'You could give me yourself.'

Margaret gasped, a sharp shock of chilly air filling her lungs. 'I beg your pardon?'

'Marry me!' he proposed abruptly, before he had a chance to think better of his presumptuous haste.

Margaret's lips parted, and John struggled not to stare at those flushed petals that were reddened by the cold, his own lips spontaneously edging nearer and wetting for want of her. It occurred to him for the hundredth time since he had met Margaret that he craved all of her: heart, body, mind and soul, not a single detail altered. As for Margaret, she had not thought he would ask her, not so soon. She had assumed that they might spend some time rebuilding their relationship, starting from the beginning, but then again, after all they had endured together, how could they ever go back? That innocence, that uncertainty, that inexperience, it could not be reclaimed, and nor would they wish it to be. They were different people now; older, wiser, and more in harmony with each other, ready to be united, to be as one. However, Margaret was fretting about one or two other misgivings that momentarily swept aside her ability to reply one way or the other.

'But how can you still want me? After everything that has happened? After everything that we have both said and done? None of it can be taken back, I know that, and so do you,' Margaret pointed out, convinced that the mistakes they had made, the misunderstandings they had shared, would be enough to rupture even the most enduring of bonds.

'I do not care what you might have done. I only care about *you*,' he disclosed, grasping one of Margaret's hands and holding it in a way that was both firm and loose, protective, but never possessive, his large fingers curling around her small ones and shielding them from the taciturn bite of the night. It reminded her of the way he had seized her hand on the day of his proposal, only, this time, she hoped he would not let go. Margaret was revived by the sensation, previously unaware of how cold she had been, and it gave her the courage she needed to know that she could find such wholehearted refuge with him by her side. She had been numb, but now she was awake to him.

'I know you, Margaret, I trust you, I believe in you. All these weeks, I have not doubted you, only myself,' he confessed, his eyes searching hers. 'I have never truly disbelieved your goodness, only my own worth when compared to your grace,' he went on, gently gripping her hand, his thumb sweeping back and forth affectionately.

'Just tell me, should I fear him?' he asked, closing his eyes and swallowing thickly as he awaited her answer, and Margaret bore witness to his handsome face, one sketched with pain on her behalf, and how she wished she could take his head in her hands, kiss him well, and quell his suspicions and sadness once and for all.

'I am not asking you to tell me who he is, or what he meant to you, only that it is over, and that I shall never have to see you in his arms again,' he flinched, the memory of it too harrowing to imagine, yet too vivid to dispel.

Continuing to study him with his closed eyes as he anticipated her response, one which would irrevocably decide his fate, Margaret smiled to herself. She considered it strange to think she held such a poetic power over another person. Only, she knew that she would not abuse her sovereignty over him, no, never. Gently prizing the scarf from his hand, she began to wrap it around his neck, ensuring it was snug and tight in the hope that the cold would never get to him again. Then, raising her hand, she pressed a palm against his cheek, and all at once, John's eyes fluttered open in disbelief. Staring deep into his soul, Margaret allowed the empathy she felt for him to pour out from her.

'I promise that you have nothing to fear from him or any other, you never have,' she said softly, and when she saw that he was about to reply, most likely to counter her pledge with another question spiked with insecurity, she bravely shuffled forwards and burrowed herself in his arms, relieved to find that they opened instinctively for her, and after a moment of hesitation, or more likely surprise, she sighed contentedly to feel his arms envelop her, drawing her further into his embrace.

'And as for being in anybody's arms, Mr Thornton, I shall always – *always*, wish to be in yours.'

John's breath shuddered in his chest to hear her speak so, words that were so delicious, that they must surely be fictitious. He was dreaming, that was it. But then as he felt her grip onto the contours of his arms and cling to him reassuringly, he sensed her sincerity, and he knew that it was real, that she was real, that this was real, that *they* were real.

Taking a finger and crooking it under her chin, John encouraged Margaret's head to tilt upwards so that she looked at him once again, her eyes brimming with wonder as they sparkled with a trust that he would never betray. He was distraught to see that her nose, her darling little nose, was turning blue, and he settled that he must get her inside soon. Before he did, he took the corner of his scarf and rubbed it lightly across the bridge, warming it and bringing it back to life. He knew he would wear her gift always, no matter what other attire he adorned, and no matter whether the skies snowed or sweltered, around his neck her scarf would proudly be.

'Well then, Miss Hale, tell me, will you not have me?' he murmured against her ear, his bristled jaw stroking her and scraping along the silky softness of Margaret's porcelain skin.

'For my friend, you mean?' Margaret smirked, and John heard himself likewise chuckling at her playfulness.

'Yes, first and foremost as your friend,' he agreed, bumping his forehead along hers.

'Always your friend. But will you not have me for your husband too?' he asked, an unmistakable fear lurking beneath the surface of his bravado. 'You shall be my first and last love —'

'Apart from our children,' she interrupted, a serious sort of earnestness to her face that made him grin, but this did not please him nearly as much as the flush that inflamed her chest to think she had mentioned such an intimate part of their future together.

'Aye, and our children,' he clarified. 'And our children's children. And our children's, children's children,' John laughed, impatient to imagine them all, dozens of Thorntons throughout the years, the embodiment of the love that one man and one woman had shared for each other in hallowed consummation.

'I will always put you first, Margaret. I will always represent and defend you, both in action and in word. I will always admire and adore you, of that I am sure. I shall never be perfect, I can never be that for you, try as I might, but I will be a good husband to you, for all the years that you bless me with your hand and your heart to have and to hold, just as I freely give you my own.'

'Yes!' Margaret cried happily as she ran her tapered fingers along his shirtsleeve, the starched cotton growing damp from all the snow that was landing on it, revealing taut muscles beneath.

'Yes, *John*, I will marry you,' she whispered, and she felt him sway against her.

With his lips grazing her ear, John could hardly speak.

'Truly, Margaret? Do not toy with me, I beg of you. I could not bear it. Are you saying you will be mine?' he had to know, his hand drifting down her back and pressing her firmly against him, terrified that she would leave him any minute now, but she was uplifted to feel that he left a gap, a breach in his embrace, which represented a chance, a choice for her to go, should she wish to, for he would never entrap her like a bird that ought to fly free.

Margaret smiled once again and mimicked his action, her hand resting on his back and holding him closer to her still, her fingers tracing his spine.

'I already am, John. I always was,' she divulged, rejoicing in the way he moaned into her hair.

Amazed by her revelation, John held onto her for dear life, afraid that she was some taunting apparition of all he yearned for, a hallucination that would soon disappear. His arms were splayed, one grasping her waist, the other caressing the base of her neck and playing with the loose wisps of brown locks that hung thereabouts. He had to be mindful not to break her, the strength of his love overpowering enough to crush her.

'Do I have your permission to call upon you tomorrow and speak with your father?' he requested impatiently, thinking that if they were quick about it, he could be a married man by his thirtieth birthday, perhaps even on the day itself if she approved.

Margaret was about to dreamily agree, lost in the jubilation of his adoration, her senses made giddy by the peppery aroma of his natural scent, but she then blinked and shook her head.

'*Tomorrow*?!' she repeated with an astonished pitch. 'But, my love, tomorrow is Christmas Day!' she reminded him, the two of them having clean forgot.

John grinned, thrilled beyond words to hear her address him with such unbridled affection. 'Aye, I know, my darling. And what better day to ask for the thing I want most in all the world?' he teased, relishing the way Margaret skewed her head in confusion, and then blushed beautifully when she understood him.

'And what might that be, Mr Thornton?' she hummed in return, draping her arms around his neck and delighting to hear him groan with euphoria to find that her hands were there once more.

John's mind evoked the memory of that chaotic morning when Margaret had flung her arms around him in defence before the rioters, and how he, consumed by concern for her safety, had not allowed himself the chance to savour the sensation, even though despite the disorientating drama of those few seconds, he had still acutely felt her touch. Oh, how John had wished with all his might at that moment that Margaret had hurled her arms around him through choice and not out of necessity. But now, such longing faded away into insignificance, because here she was again, with no threat of terror to overrule her actions, her arms around his neck of their own free accord, and there he hoped they would remain for the rest of their lives as Mr and Mrs Thornton.

The snow, which had ceased in its heavenly sprinkling during their avowals, once again began to fall around them. Reaching into his coat that lay on her shoulders, John retrieved the stem of mistletoe that he had stuffed in there earlier during his heated departure. Holding it high above their heads, he gazed down at her as she gazed up at him, their eyes twinkling like the stars that blessed them this night. With their lips creeping nearer, he smiled, and she did too, all before he sweetly whispered:

'Well, Miss Hale…what I want is very simple, and very near, and believe me when I say that it is very special, for it is very, *very* dear.'

Chapter Twelve

Hark! I am Home!

It was the following Christmas Eve that John Thornton made his way through the sleeping ginnels of Milton as swiftly as his legs would carry him, the scene silvered by the frost that had blown its icy breath across the town. Stifling a yawn, he thrust his hands into his coat pockets, but not before he tightened the scarf around his neck, not only to warm his body, but his spirits too, this loop made of love never failing to bring him comfort and cheer, and he needed it tonight, sorely so.

He was cold. He was tired. He was hungry. But most of all, he was impatient!

It was getting late, and still his day was far from over, even if it were drawing close to a most contented conclusion. Earlier this afternoon, John had stood by the railings of the boat that brought him back from France, his eyes squinting as they combed the horizon, minding the coastline for the landmark sight that welcomed many a weary wanderer back to the shores of England, the white cliffs of Dover. With an irascible scowl, his restlessness only began to abate when a rocky wall of chalk appeared in the distance, the sight becoming ever more prominent as they sailed towards land. It had not been until he firmly stepped foot back on English soil, that he breathed a heavy sigh of relief. As he boarded his train bound north, John had tried to ignore the many miles that separated him from his home, preferring to dwell on how grateful he would be to once again be back where he belonged. John had not yet returned to the house, instead, he had chosen to head straight from the station to where his feet compelled him now. Part of him chided himself for having not made more of an effort to hail a Hackney cab to both alleviate and hasten the last leg of his journey, but his long limbs needed a good-old stretch, and carriages were few and far between on the night before Christmas, so he may as well walk.

Grumbling, and watching as his breath turned to steam a few inches in front of his nose before scattering like an ethereal mist on his face, John wished that he had not gone away at all, especially now, at this time of year, and with everything that he would be leaving behind. However, he knew it had been, if not the right thing to do, then at least the prudent one, and in time, the profitable one, not that such petty trivialities mattered to him these days, for the materialistic irrelevance of pounds and profit were nothing compared to the mortal and moral peace he had found within. No, John wished that he had remained in Milton, but alas, she had told him to go, she had insisted, reminding him that it was the most wonderful thing that had happened to Marlborough

Mills since he had been appointed its master six years before, and therefore, he would regret it if he did not take this intrepid chance. So he had done as he was told, just as he had done for the past twelve months, ever since she had taken charge of him and vowed to care for him for the rest of their days.

John smiled to himself. She was always right. *Always*.

When he finally turned the corner onto that oh-so-familiar street, John could feel his heart thumping in his chest as it sensed the setting and its proximity to its other half, and so it thrummed a steadfast beat as it called out to its mate: '*Hark! I am home!*' With a hastened pace, he reached the end of the road, both literally and figuratively speaking, and so John came to stand in front of a house, one that was tall and thin, residing in a tucked-away part of town, rendering it inconsequential to most, but to him, it currently held the most treasured wonders in all the world. Coming to an abrupt halt, John looked up purposefully, his eyes fixing upon a window with no hint of shyness, but absolute intent, and there he remained, no longer hoping that he would find what he wanted there, but trusting that it would be so. The window was trimmed with a border of snow and a row of clinkerbells that glittered with their frosty icing, affecting it to look like a picture frame that promised to reveal the prettiest picture of all.

In time, his faith was rewarded, because a few moments later, while he maintained his stalwart vigil, John spied a figure gracefully shifting behind the glass, and all at once, all of his previous tensions faded away, along with the cold that had bothered him, a sense of gratified joy warming him through and through. He knew he really should go indoors, but John did not make to leave his lookout post, but rested awhile to marvel at this sight, overwhelmed by an inexplicable serenity to think of how much had changed since that sacred night, one year ago, when he had looked up at that very same window. It had pained him then to think of all that stood between him and the one inside, partitioned by a transparent barrier as they were, this unworldly angel existing high above him, out of reach from his unworthy grasp, and how he had longed to shatter that impediment between them that had been founded on nothing more than a distinction of class, a division of background, and the disillusionment of misunderstandings.

And, *oh*! – how they had shattered it, together.

With his quickening breath catching in his throat, he watched as the figure drew nearer, their identity frustratingly concealed by a thin curtain, but it mattered not, because he knew who they were, he knew them very well indeed, better than he knew himself.

It was *a* woman, *the* woman, *his* woman — what a woman!

Fumbling with a blanket in her hands, she draped it around something in her arms which she held before her, gently rocking it back and forth and up and down, her head bent low to admire what she kept close to her heart, and even from where he stood outside, John's soul hummed jubilantly to see the overflowing adoration in her eyes, ones that were the same colour as his scarf, his most prized earthly possession.

Again, John should have moved, but he was so enthralled that he found he could not, uncomplainingly captivated by this sweet enchantress' spell. He lingered there still, and watched as she walked towards the window, and peering up, she pulled the curtain aside, her gaze travelling along the street, searching for something with unwavering focus, the skin creasing at the edges of her eyes in dissatisfaction when she could not see —

She stopped. She stilled. She smiled.

John could scarcely draw breath, overpowered as he was by such wholesome awe.

As her eyes returned to the doorstep, they brushed past him, but then they scurried back, and after a few fleeting seconds of contemplation as she studied the lone figure in the street, her lips parted, and her mouth made a pretty oval shape of recognition to discover him there, her visage one of rejoicing. Taking off his hat, he tipped it towards her, and placing his hand over his mouth, John kissed it once and swept it up towards her, an enamoured dispatch, a moistened message, sent from one lover to another. The woman laughed merrily at this, and reaching out, she swiped the air and snatched at it with a closed fist before drawing it towards her and clutching it to her breast. She then lifted a hand to the window and laid it against the glass, and there, her fingers gently tapped their greeting, all before they turned and twitched eagerly, summoning him to come inside at once.

John did not need to be asked twice.

Near enough running up the steps, John slipped and skidded on the ice, his knee knocking into the railing with a throbbing blow, but he did not care tuppence. Instead, he took hold of the handle and pushed open the door that had been left off the latch for him, relieved to feel the rush of warm air that shrouded him as he cocooned himself within this haven of peaceful tranquillity, this veritable hibernacle. It was as he was removing his coat that he spotted the bunches of festive posies hanging from the ceiling, and with a nostalgic smile gracing his lips, he stretched upwards and carefully liberated a cluster of mistletoe, placing it in his pocket for safekeeping. Presently, a familiar face emerged from the kitchen and bustled along to meet him, their trusty rolling pin waving in his direction by way of welcome.

'Here you are, then,' resounded a cheerful voice, one which he could not quite get used to addressing him with affability, having been previously accustomed to hearing it scoff at him with poorly disguised disapproval in the past.

'We were starting to worry about you,' they added, a trace of matronly admonishment to their tone as they took his mufflements and hung them up on his usual peg. On seeing him shudder and chafe his hands together to keep them from turning to ice, they tutted noisily and were quick to usher him towards the parlour, shooing him like a stray cat that they intended on smothering with their mithering.

'Now you go on in there and rest yourself by the fire. Your dinner is on the stove, I kept some back for you, good-old-proper English mutton, so I will bring it along shortly, and no doubt she will be down any minute now to see you,' they prophesied, their arm wafting upwards as they flapped a dusting cloth about the place, cross to see that they had missed a spot earlier. John grinned, although he did not do as he was bidden, but lingered in the doorway to the parlour, waiting for the opportune moment to sneak upstairs.

'Thank you, Dixon,' he replied, his gratitude rewarded by an acknowledging bob of her head before she ambled back to the kitchen, muttering something under her breath about how she was going to need to fatten him up again after a week of eating nothing but snails, not that John had ever eaten a snail, of course.

Once he was sure she was gone, and filled with a restless urgency that he could not contain, John was ready to daringly disobey Dixon and continue on up the stairs, but he was once again halted when he sensed a movement behind him, shortly followed by a hand landing on his arm and squeezing there in jolly salutation.

'There you are, my dear boy!' said the owner of the very same hand, one that was wrinkled and crinkled with the tell-tale creases of age. 'I am glad to see you are back with us, safe and sound at last.'

Suppressing a huff of mild frustration, John twisted round to see Mr Hale standing beside him. Nevertheless, his impatience was short-lived, for as much as he was keen to get up those stairs, he was gratified beyond words to see his esteemed friend again, and gladdened further to see him looking so well, the past year having heartily restored the enthusiasm and energy he had temporarily lost following the death of his wife.

'Richard,' John replied, thinking on how he must sit down soon with the man who was still his tutor to discuss the tome of Socrates he had been reading while away.

Mr Hale bobbed up and down on the soles of his feet as he nodded pensively, the profound significance of tonight not having escaped him.

'And here we are again,' said he, looking about him at the evocative scene, 'another Christmas Eve together,' he reminisced, shaking his head to think that a whole year had passed since the last one.

At this, John's restiveness was appeased, and he smiled, a small, private smile. 'Aye,' he agreed wistfully, 'and how much has changed since then?'

Chapter Thirteen

Are You Happy?

It was during the small hours of Christmas morning the previous year, that John had begrudgingly trudged home from the Hale's, a walk that was laden with the depressive knowledge that it took him ever further away from his sweetheart. When he eventually came to stalk under the shadow of the factory that stretched high into the black night, its lofty chimneys sticking up and spearing the darkness like black spikes, John pushed open the mill gate that groaned grumpily to be woken up so late. Being sure to lock it behind him, he considered what he should do to pass the long and lonely hours until he saw Margaret again. He knew he should go to bed, but his mind was too alive, too alert, so he determined that it would be pointless to spend his time tossing and turning, a senseless exercise that would only serve to add to his exhaustion. Perhaps he should go to his library and read, but then again, he knew he would be unable to concentrate, so that would likewise be a futile effort. In the end, he landed on the notion of starting to plan their wedding. He and Margaret had not discussed it, he did not know when and where she would like to become Mrs John Thornton, and he would naturally bow down to whatever she wished, but he was too excited to do nothing, so he would have to content himself with drafting some initial thoughts for their nuptials to show her tomorrow, the only detail that really mattered being that she marry him.

Once he was indoors and free of his outer-garments, other than his scarf, that is, John crept along the passageway to his study, not wishing to disturb anyone, acutely aware that his heavy steps could echo in such a large house, one that was apparently so substantial in its proportions, that their staircases alone were wider than the Hale's drawing room, or so his sister had informed him repeatedly. Taking care to walk at an abnormally slow pace, John skulked past the dining room, and as he did, he was arrested by a dim light flickering on the dining table. When he peered inside, he was obliged to blink in partial blindness as he was met by the weak light of a few paltry lamps which were doing a half-hearted job of illuminating the landscape. Sharpening his gaze, John perceived that the pathetic spattering of lights glowed with lackadaisical laziness, their oily flames lulled into slumber by the cloak of gloom that was cast about the place. Nevertheless, despite the obscurity before him, John spied a shape adorned in black sitting across the way, and he realised with a pang of guilt that his mother must have waited up for him. Ah! Of course she had, she had said she would, and she was a woman dependable for her word.

It was at this juncture that John was overcome by a niggling uncertainty. Should he share his good news with his mother? He had originally judged it best to bide his time and be patient, to deny himself the right to revel in his joy until he had spoken with his prospective father-in-law. He and Margaret had not specifically agreed on such an arrangement, but to his own mind, John appreciated that he had been impulsive thus far in his court of Margaret, always funnelling ahead without thinking, so it was time that he reined himself in and conducted himself with the same level-headed consideration that he intended to apply to his marriage. After all, his mother held formidable views when it came to his feelings for *that woman!*, as she would doubtless call her, so he did not wish to give her the opportunity to cast aspersions on his future happiness, nor the sincerity of his fiancée's love for him, not when he wanted to savour this feeling of blissful contentment that still flooded him. However, it had been no use. From the moment John had stepped into the room, his mother could see it written across his face, one she could read like a book.

'I see,' she had opened with an unsteady breath that shuddered with a minor dose of shock as she laid down her sewing, wary that she might prick herself at such a momentous moment. However, it was indeed minor, because if Mrs Thornton were honest, she had been preparing herself for this eventuality for the past five hours, a precipitous change in circumstances which she had come to realise was inevitable. She had seen the earnestness in her son's face as he readied to leave for his evening engagement, and so, as she had stood in a corner of the Trafalgar House ballroom, absorbed in lonely contemplation, unconscious of the festive frivolities that danced around her at the Latimer's party, she was coming to terms with the knowledge that, one way or another, the fate of her son's love for that woman would be decided tonight.

'We only arrived back an hour ago ourselves,' she clarified, grateful that her daughter had been worn out from all the revelry and gone to bed, rather than having been present, only to act as a gawking spectator to this extraordinary final act in which a mother stepped aside as the first in her son's affections, giving way to another who would become his undisputed companion and confidant.

'Still, I had thought you might be home to meet us. I had wondered why you were so late, but I see now where you have been for so long and why,' she went on, looking him up and down and noting his new scarf, a rather handsome raiment, she had to concede.

'She said yes, then,' his mother deduced, returning her attention to her sewing, unable to look at him when she spoke, her words a statement rather than a question.

'Yes.'

His reply had been concise and unapologetically honest.

He knew that it had been imprudent, but John could not hide anything from his mother, he never could. And besides, why should he? He was not ashamed. He had done nothing wrong. He was in love, and the woman he held dear in his heart loved him in return. It was not every man who could boast such blessed luck in this life, so John was ready to proclaim his good fortune far and wide. Furthermore, he had spent most of his life negating his needs for the sake of other's wants, but no more. He would not repress how he felt. He would not refrain from asserting what he yearned for, and that, was Margaret.

In the wake of his confession, there had been an excruciating pause, during which Mrs Thornton had expected a storm to rage inside her, and she was ready for it, fully prepared to fight it, to allay it, to overpower it, armed with the fortitude of her innate northern grit. But alas, no such tempest came, and instead, all she could feel was the gentle rushing of still waters pouring into her tired soul and nourishing it with a restful sense of peace.

'Well then, that is that,' was all she could mutter, for what more was there to say?

At first, John had been disappointed that his mother had not congratulated him, but then he supposed that he ought to be grateful that she had not said more, that she had not, in fact, counselled him to reconsider, telling him that he was erroneous in his choice of wife, and advising him in the strongest possible language to give up on Miss Margaret Hale once and for all. Consequently, nodding his head in resignation, John had quietly retreated, deciding after all that he would go to his chamber and try to sleep, since he knew he had a busy day ahead of him tomorrow. However, he abruptly stopped as she called out: '*John?*'

He did not turn round, not fully, but merely crooked his head over his shoulder, and even though he could not see her, he could sense the vacillation in his mother's voice.

'Are you happy?' she asked after a fraught respite of contemplation.

'Yes,' he replied straight away. He did not need to think. He knew his answer. He had never been happier.

'Good,' she said at last, and Mrs Thornton let out a breath that she had been holding deep inside her for fifteen years, one filled with anxiety and anger on behalf of her son and all he had endured.

She was *so tired - so tired of being whirled on through all these phases of life, in which nothing abides, no creature, no place; it is like the circle in which the victims of earthly passion eddy continually.*

It was time. It was finally time to let go.

'Then I am happy, too…for both of you.'

It was only a few hours later that John had awoken at first light and set off for Crampton. It was early, too early, far too early to make a civilised call. Unsure of what to do with himself, he had stalked the neighbouring streets, marching up and down and up again as he passed an hour or two in fitful unrest, drawing attention to himself as many an onlooker observed him with more than a mite of curiosity, each of them speculating (a word he hated), as to what the Master of Marlborough Mills was doing out and about at this time of the morning, and in this part of town, not to mention behaving so very oddly. Still, there were one or two gossipmongers who winked at each other, tittle-tattling as they passed a plate of mince pies around, whispering with scandalous twitters that he had apparently been seen with that pretty parson's daughter the previous evening, out in the dark, all alone, the pair intertwined in each other's arms while their mouths made merry with a passionate kiss.

As for John, he did not give a fig what people thought, not today. Besides, he had other more pressing concerns on his mind. On one hand, he was giddy with gladness, his heart as light as a bird to think that he would see his beloved soon and their engagement would be made official, transforming what had once seemed like an impossible dream into a reality. On the other hand, just like that, he was beset by a horrible dread that gnawed away at his optimism.

What if Mr Hale said no?

He wouldn't. He may. He couldn't. He might.

This uncertainty filled John with a bedevilling apprehension that he had been rash in informing his mother of his good news before it had been approved by his intended's guardian. What a fool he would look if permission were denied them, how distraught he would be, and then what? Could he change his friend's mind and encourage Mr Hale to appreciate his worth? Could he convince him that he was a fitting choice of suitor for his daughter? Could he persuade him that he would care for Margaret and love her like no man ever could? Or would they need to postpone until she turned of age to marry without his blessing? John did not like this idea one bit. This would keep him from Margaret for nearly two years, and even though John would willingly wait for her, he was impatient to end his bachelorhood and take her as his bride as soon as possible. Not only that, but he would be loath to war with Mr Hale, and as for Margaret, she would naturally not wish to disobey her father and fracture her relationship with her sole-surviving parent, even if it meant she could be happy. And what if her family tried to dissuade her of her choice in the meantime? Margaret might even be sent off to London to live with her aunt again, and no doubt Lennox would be prowling about, and if not him, then she was still bound to meet a man who was ten times more handsome, talented and wealthy than John, and then where would that leave him?

Heartbroken. Humiliated. And with another man taking his place as Margaret's husband.

Needless to say that it was not long before John's confidence unravelled and lay undone on the pavement before him. In the end, he determined that there was only one thing to be done, and that was to make haste to the Hale's so that his fate could be decided once and for all.

'*Come poor little heart! be cheery and brave,*' he whispered to his own tender heart that cried out to Margaret. '*We'll be a great deal to one another, if we are thrown off and left desolate.*'

John walked briskly, his strides near enough breaking out into a run, and springing up the steps of the Crampton house, he was about to knock on the door, his fist quivering with impatience. However, he quickly found that he had no need, because it opened before he had the chance, and there Margaret stood to greet him. He was instantly halted, and standing back, John was taken aback, and he let out a trembling breath of reprieve, because in that instant, he realised something. Never once during all of his agitated hours since they had said their bittersweet goodbye and goodnight had John doubted the constancy of Margaret's love for him. Here he was, afraid that his mother would caution him, that Mr Hale would reject him, that his sister would laugh at him, but not once had he disbelieved his darling girl. It was incredible. After months of being afflicted by an uncertainty about if and when and why she would come to care for him, all of that insecurity had vanished overnight, never to return to plague him again. As he regarded her with her cheeks flushed with the anticipation of their imminent reunion, John knew that Margaret had shared a similar night. She had been waiting for him, hoping that he would come to her as soon as he could, and so he would brave this day for her sake as well as his, refusing to let her down.

Stepping aside, Margaret accompanied him into the house, and after she had taken his things, which had involved lovingly prying his scarf away from a reluctant John, since he did not want to let it go, they had stared into each other's eyes, bumping into this and that as they made their way to the parlour. When she pushed the door open, Margaret quietly confided to him that she had told her father nothing, and when Mr Hale looked up, his glasses fell from his face in patent surprise.

'*John*!' he had exclaimed. 'My word!' he affixed, still at a loss for words and struggling to manage more than two at a time.

'What brings you here?' he asked, assuming that John must have forgotten something from the preceding evening, either that, or he had some relevant news to impart that could not be delayed. After John and Margaret had glanced at each other furtively, she slowly slipped out of the room, but not before silently mouthing to her fiancé that she trusted that all would be well, giving him the bolstering courage he needed.

Once she had left them to it, John turned to face Mr Hale, his tutor staring at him with an expression of sheer bewilderment, still awaiting an answer, perturbed by his pupil's attendance at his house on Christmas Day. The young man's nervousness must have shown, because Mr Hale then ventured to comment on how pale his friend looked, even going so far as to question whether he was ill. John shook his head in vehement dispute and fastened his hands behind his back like a wayward schoolboy who had been dragged before the headmaster. Swallowing a thick ball of anxiety that had become lodged in his throat before he choked on it, he muttered something incoherent.

'What was that?' Mr Hale enquired, straining to hear him, causing him to tug on his ears to make way for sound to pass through more easily.

'I...I have come to ask, sir, if – if I might...if you would be willing to consider giving your consent...bestowing your blessing...'

'I am sorry,' the tutor said, shaking his head lamely, 'I am afraid that I am going to have to ask you to speak up.'

'I want to marry your daughter!' John blurted out.

There was understandably a self-conscious intermission while Mr Hale's mouth fell open like a codfish, and he regarded John with eyes that darted across his features, examining him charily, trying to work out whether this was a hoax, but if it was, he could not understand it any better.

'You mean Margaret?'

'Yes.'

'But why?'

'Because I am extremely fond of her.'

'I beg your pardon?'

'Because I have feelings for her.'

'Come again?'

'I said I love her!'

The preceding lines had been spoken in quick succession, both men hardly knowing what was being said and by whom, only, John, he had delivered his last line with confidence, remaining bold in his unswerving sincerity. Even so, he wished that he could express himself better. This was a significant occasion, one that he would never experience again, and he sorely wanted to do himself justice, and more importantly, to do his love for Margaret justice. Licking his parched lips, he cursed himself inwardly for being so inarticulate when it came to adequately conveying the truth and tenderness that he harboured in his heart.

'Mar – Miss Hale and I, we love each other, and we would like your permission to marry…as soon as possible.'

It was not that John was rude enough to consult his watch at this point, but still, he could have sworn that Mr Hale gawked at him for an eternity, until, finally, the master of the house had to sit down, the shock of it all having rather knocked the puff out of his sails. He knew that he was getting on, but he was not quite at a dizzying age yet, although this morning was leaving him feeling well and truly dizzy.

'*You and Margaret*?' he reiterated, as if the very suggestion was fantastic. 'But you do not like each other. You never have,' he noted, unsure of how his pupil had forgotten this fundamental fact.

John grumbled, his mind racing to consider how to describe the complicated series of events that had brought one man and one woman together, two people who may never have otherwise met without the intervening hand of fate, providence having meddled with their life stories, and thus arranged for two souls to cross paths so that they could court their true and better halves. But then again, how could someone explain the inexplicable? So John deemed it best just to speak the simple truth.

'I grant that it may have appeared so in the past, but that has all changed,' he began, not ashamed of the history he shared with his beloved.

'I see now that it was a façade, a way for us to mask our feelings for each other, feelings that were strong and overwhelming, unlike anything we had ever felt before, both of us untrained and untried in the ways of love. We did not quite know what to do with ourselves, of how to be around each other, of how to tell each other how we actually felt, so we sparred, when in truth, all we wanted was to be with one another. '

Mr Hale's eyes widened in further astonishment. 'I see,' he exhaled. 'And you say my daughter loves you? I take it, then, that you have already asked her?'

'Yes,' John admitted, shuffling uneasily on the spot to have been caught out on this point, fractious at having been remiss for a second time in following the expectations of polite society by not speaking to Mr Hale first, once again causing him to mistrust his gentlemanly conduct. Nonetheless, Margaret would not have thanked him for his attentiveness to propriety, because that would mean that the wants of others ranked above her own, and she would have given John short shrift, reminding him that it was her who was marrying him, not her father, so he was better asking her directly, which he had.

'When?' Mr Hale questioned, still amazed by the astounding situation.

John replied initially with a nervous cough. 'Last – last night,' choosing to omit one small detail, which was that he had in fact asked her, or tried to ask her, long before.

Mr Hale nearly fell out of his chair. '*Last night?*' he repeated, unconvinced as to when and where this all-important tête-à-tête could possibly have taken place during their evening gathering. He himself had been there all the time, had he not? Trawling through his memory, he established that yes, he had, other than that brief period when Margaret had shown John to the door to wish him farewell.

'And she has consented to your offer? Your request for her hand?'

'She has,' John confirmed unequivocally, although his typically terse mouth could not help but twist upwards at the corners, the man still as pleased and proud as punch to think that she had agreed to be his wife, his woman, his world entire.

'I see,' Mr Hale re-joined after a lengthy recess in which he tried to regulate his pulse, his heart not as robust as it used to be. He was obliged to lightly smack his cheek to ensure that he was indeed awake, this whole conversation beginning to feel like a surreal dream. And yet, if he paused to reflect, it all made perfect sense. It would explain why the two young people had been behaving so strangely of late. It was not that they had been indifferent to each other, no-no, it was that they had been in the midst of falling in love.

'In that case, you had better send her in so that I can offer you both my congratulations,' he said at last with a spent shrug of his shoulders, unsure of what else he was supposed to do at a time like this.

John blinked. 'Is that it?'

His partner, in what had been a hither and thither exchange, had but a moment before been rising from his chair, but he promptly sat back down, sensing that this interview was not yet over. Taking off his glasses and wiping them with one of his late wife's handkerchiefs, wondering what on earth she would have made of all of this, he tried to understand John's reluctance to accept his pending father-in-law's acceptance of Margaret's acceptance of his proposal of marriage.

'Excuse me?' he queried. 'I do not quite follow, dear man.'

'I mean, do you not have more questions for me?' John checked earnestly, thinking of the numerous interrogating questions he would have for any future man who wanted to so much as come within a hundred miles of one of his daughters (he planned on having several children), let alone marry one of them.

Again, Mr Hale had to ponder on this. 'Such as?' he prompted, in need of a suggestion or two.

John blustered, raking through the weeds of his restless mind and scolding himself for his incessant inability to govern his tongue. He was well accustomed to managing over a hundred men every darn day, so why could he not manage himself today?

'Well, I suppose such as what my intentions are, whether I intend to make her happy, and whether I can provide for her and our family whom I trust will join us soon enough.'

Smiling in understanding, Mr Hale slapped his legs and stood up once again.

'I have no need to ask any such thing,' he settled, 'because I already know the answer.'

Coming to stand in front of the young man, he took his hands in his and shook them cordially.

'You are a good man, John, possibly the most honest, hard-working and honourable man I have ever had the good fortune to meet. In truth, I have wanted this for a long time, almost as long as I have known you, but I dared not believe it would come to pass. You and Margaret may have your disagreements, but at heart, you are one and the same. I cannot think of anyone whom I would rather see her spend the rest of her life with, and I know, that when I am gone, she will be well cared for. If she loves you, truly loves you, John, then that is good enough for me.'

'Thank you,' John replied faintly, moved to the very core by Mr Hale's faith in him.

The two men shared a meaningful glance, the sort that a father and son might share. Mr Hale was about ready to pour himself a medicinal glass of brandy to calm his nerves of both exhilaration and exhaustion after the import of the past five minutes, but first, he went to the door to invite his daughter to join them, well aware that her ear was pressed up against the frame on the other side, listening intently. But before he did, he let out a lively chuckle, calling over his shoulder, 'And besides, it is Margaret. If she has decided she wants to marry you, then who are you or I to try and stop her?'

When her father opened the door to a room erupting with laughter, it came as no surprise that Margaret stumbled in and toppled straight into John, her back striking his side, and she nearly whimpered, for he was of solid build. Thankfully for her, John was quick about it, and he caught her from falling, his fiancée clasped close in his arms for a fleeting interval, affording him the prized chance to admire her beautiful blush before reluctantly letting her go, not that he would of if they had been alone, wishing to enfold her in his embrace for as long as she chose to stay there. Clearing his throat and straightening his jacket, John then resumed a more formal tone and informed Mr and Miss Hale that they were both invited to Marlborough House for Christmas luncheon, and Margaret beamed to see the hope in his face that they would accept, which, of course, they did.

Lunch had been an interesting affair, to put it mildly. It had begun with the newly engaged couple standing awkwardly before their family members, each one regarding them with their own variety of thinly-veiled disbelief. As for John's sister, Fanny had experienced an unprecedented degree of silence. She had barely managed to utter a single word the whole afternoon, strange for someone who was a practised church-bell, but then again, she had no need to, her expression had said it all. Sitting across from her brother and future sister-in-law, she had gawped at them agog with eyes that near-enough popped out of her head, spluttering loudly every time the pair whispered in each other's ears. She had never seen her brother smile so much, a right gigglemug he was that day. There had even been one occasion when she had dropped her napkin, so ducking to retrieve it, she had almost shrieked to spy that they were holding hands beneath the table, their fingers interlacing as their feet knocked together playfully.

However, despite the initial discomfort that had discomposed them all, the five of them had passed a pleasant day together. The dinner itself had been a feast fit for a king, the spread laden with all manner of meats and preserves, fruits and pies, John having stipulated that every festive treat conceivable be prepared for the future mistress, leaving his poor cook in need of forty winks by the time the last course had been sent upstairs. After they had dined, the merry party retired to a glass of sherry for the women and port for the men, and listened to Fanny's piano recital, shortly before her brother had suggested they play some parlour games as an alternative, and so they proceeded to indulge in a round of charades, leaving Margaret pleasantly surprised to find her fiancé so agreeable, his liveliness infectious to them all. After a while, Margaret had gradually felt her shyness ebb away, and John had sat back and beamed with pride to see her talking freely in his house, making herself at home in what would become their home together, one filled with the light of love and laughter.

By the time dusk had settled on the town, each of them had come to appreciate that while the north and the south maintained their differences, they enjoyed their similarities too, and when united, they could bring forth harmony. When the time had come to part ways, and John had summoned the Thornton's carriage to take the Hales back to Crampton, Mrs Thornton had kissed Margaret on the cheek, and with her lips pressed close to her ear, she had welcomed the girl to the family. After wishing Margaret and her father goodbye, as well as promising to call upon them at a more reasonable time the following morning, John had returned to join his mother and sister, the two of them sitting quietly to mull over the events of the day. Standing before them with folded arms, John let his eyes flit between them guardedly, and then opening his arms wide to invite their derision so that he might get it over and done with, he announced: '*Well*? Let's have it then!'

He waited patiently for their retorts, assuming that they would ridicule him in some way, but neither did. Instead, his sister simply declared, 'She is too good for you,' and as for his mother, she smiled, and added, 'She was born to be a Thornton.'

Chapter Fourteen

Two Turtle Doves

Returning to the here and now, John glanced up the stairs, and his father-in-law was touched to detect the longing in his son-in-law's face.

'How are they?' John asked with tender reverence.

'They have missed you,' Mr Hale told him reassuringly. 'They have been watching and waiting for you all day.'

It was then that John heard the sound of footsteps, and looking up, he saw the flash of a red skirt swish past his vision.

'Margaret, dearest, look who is here,' her father proclaimed, reminding John once again of the year before, only, now, the reply that floated down to greet his ears was sweeter by far.

'Coming, John, coming!' a voice called back in cheerful reply.

A moment later, there she was, gliding down the stairs. Margaret did not hurry this time, but rather, with cautious steps, she made her way to him, until, at last, the wife stood before her husband, her cheeks rosy with the pleasure of seeing him again.

'Well-well,' said Mr Hale, his gaze shifting between them in confelicity, bearing witness to the adoration they clearly felt for one another. 'Here we all are again! I am quite sure you shall want some time alone, so I will say goodnight and see you both in the morning.' He was beholden that they did not intend to return to Marlborough House until tomorrow, giving him the delight of sharing in a scrumptious Christmas breakfast with the three of them. And with that, he left them to it.

Reunited once more after far too long apart, John and Margaret trailed slowly towards the parlour, her head on his shoulder, his arm around her waist, the two of them relieved to be alone at last, or that is, almost alone. Smiling at one another knowingly, they glanced down to admire what she cradled in her arms, and there lay a tiny treasure.

Gabriel Thornton had been welcomed into the world on the first day of December 1855, a happy and healthy baby boy with black hair and blue eyes. The seed of his conception had been sewn mere weeks after their wedding, which had taken place in mid-February, on the very day his parents had first met a year before. John had been fervently reluctant to leave his wife and babe so soon after he had been born, but Margaret had persuaded him to go, saying that the sooner he went, the sooner he would be back, and then they could spend Christmas together as a family. Giving in, John had ensured that his travel plans and business affairs were as efficient as possible, guaranteeing that he was not away from Milton for more than six days, and he had been true to his word, not a minute less, not a minute more. He had been pleased to meet his brother-in-law while abroad, Frederick having journeyed to France with the express purpose of introducing himself, affording John the curious chance of coming face-to-face with the man he had hated for months, amazed to think that he could ever have nurtured such loathing for someone who was unmistakably a Hale.

At any rate, it so happened that a week before John's departure, his sister had married a fellow cotton master of the town, a Mr Watson, and because she wanted to ensure that her new home was in order, she had stipulated that her mother must come and stay with her while she set up house. Mrs Thornton had agreed half-heartedly, and while Margaret had been given the option of either residing with Mrs Watson or remaining at Marlborough House on her own, she had preferred to come to Crampton to keep her father company, and so here she was, living in her old house, the difference being that she was awaiting the return of her husband to take her home again.

'How I have missed you both,' he whispered, his forehead lightly bumping against hers, his lips grazing her temple and leaving a sweeping kiss there.

With his hands extended out in eager longing, John took the baby from his mother while she left the room to fetch something, and the little lad wriggled to feel the change, sensing that he was now in arms that were not slim of shape and smooth of skin, but tremendously strong. He looked so very calm and cosy as he slept, and John supposed that Margaret had not long finished nursing him, thus explaining her delay in coming downstairs. Opening his eyes, two oceans of cloudy blue, Gabriel peered up at his father, and after regarding him with a series of drowsy blinks, his mouth twitched in recognition, and he gurgled happily. John's heart soared to look upon his son, overcome to think that he may never have known the soulful rhapsody of fatherhood if he had never met and married Margaret. Yawning, the little lamb stretched his arms, and reaching out, he grabbed hold of John's finger and tightened his grip, the man marvelling to see how miniscule the infant's hands were compared to his own sizeable ones. Margaret had been right in what she said a year ago. This house had needed a child to rekindle the joy it had lost, new life ushering in a new hope to lay to rest the sadness inflicted by the death and divisions it had endured.

When she returned a short while later, Margaret peeked down at Gabriel and cooed, her heart fit to burst with love for this little lamb who was his parent's pride and joy. She had left to retrieve John's scarf, and swathing her son in it, the couple watched in awe as their baby smiled in his sleep, content in the knowledge that he was unconditionally and unreservedly loved. With quiet treads, John and Margaret sat down on a settee that rested beside the

Christmas tree, and gazing up at it dreamily, they studied it in wonderment. Both of them knew that they ought to talk about his time abroad and the various successes it had brought, a blessed security for their future, but that could wait, for there were far more important matters to discuss first.

'There are more ornaments this year,' he remarked.

'Yes,' she confirmed, 'they are from your workers.'

Inspecting the tree, John took in all the decorations, big and small, that had been hand-crafted, each one more beautiful than the last with their glass, embroidery and flecks of paint.

'These are a testament to you, young master,' observed John, amused by the way the lad burrowed his head into his father's chest. 'And you, wife,' he added, gazing at Margaret fondly, noting how she was wearing the same dress that she had worn last year, secretly surprised that she could fit it, her hips and chest having swelled most pleasingly in recent months. Then, with his voice suddenly taking on a more serious air, he continued.

'My workers have never been so at peace, and that is down to you,'

Margaret furrowed her nose adorably. '*Me*?'

'Aye, you,' he nodded most assuredly. 'You are one of them now.'

'One of your workers?'

'No! A Miltoner. You are one of us now, you are a Milton woman, Margaret, you were always meant to be. You understand the people of this town, you appreciate them, you sustain them, and for that, they cherish you wholeheartedly. You have been such a marvel this past year. We cannot forget the school and hospital you helped bring about. I thought you were misguided in wanting to open them as you did, but as always, you were right, and they are thriving, proving to me and everyone hereabouts how sorely they were needed. And not only that, but you have been a godsend in helping me to make the mill what it is, rescuing it from the brink of collapse with your initiatives, and trusting me with Mr Bell's endowment for our wedding gift. The mill is yours now, Margaret, ever since he signed it over to you, and it has been an honour to make it a place you can be proud of, somewhere you are not ashamed to be associated with or live next to. Somewhere that you are not ashamed for your husband to make a living to support our family. You are a miracle, Margaret, not only for me, but for all of us here, and I want you to know it,' he said, cupping her cheek and sniffing sentimentally.

His wife had been listening to him intently, forever transfixed by that baritone timbre that caressed her soul with its unparalleled warmth.

'That is kind of you to say, John, but it is not entirely true, is it?' she chuckled, lifting one of his hands and kissing it, the hair on his knuckles tickling her nose, and she sighed dotingly to hear him moan blissfully.

'Do you not see? It is all down to you, dearest. You are the very best master in this town, you always were, I always knew you to be. You are a good man, husband of mine, the very best of that too, otherwise, I would never have married you, and as for your workers, these gifts,' she said, lifting her eyes to the tree, 'they are for you. Why, you might ask? Because you are held in the highest regard, you are respected above all others, dear heart. I just wish you would let yourself accept it.'

John was about to reply, perhaps to argue that in that case, he must be the most beloved bulldog in all of Darkshire, but then he spotted something sitting under the tree with his name scribbled on it in an elegant hand he knew well, given that he had seen it on many an affectionate note left on his study or office desk.

'What is that?' he asked nosily, a childish fizz of excitement taking hold of him.

Margaret grinned, and slipping her hand beneath the lowly branches to reclaim it, she handed it to her husband.

'I suppose you should really wait for tomorrow,' she admitted, 'but then again, I think you and I have our own tradition of giving gifts on Christmas Eve, do we not?'

Smirking at her teasing, John gladly took it from her, and tearing open the parcel-paper, two items fell onto his lap. They were both blue. Both soft. Both beautiful. Both —

'Gloves!' he exclaimed, holding them up to look them over, finding that they were an exact match for his scarf.

'Yes!' Margaret giggled, clapping her hands together gleefully. 'I know they are not nearly as fashionable as your smart leather ones, but I thought with all the bits and pieces I was making for this little man,' she explained, tickling Gabriel's chin, 'then my other Mr Thornton deserved something too.'

John threw his head back and laughed heartily. 'Thank you, love. I could not have asked for anything better,' he acknowledged, thinking on how he venerated it whenever Margaret kissed his hands, something she often did, whenever he was feeling overburdened, even if such occurrences were growing fewer by the day. However, now, he could encase his hands in these gloves, knowing that she had crafted them with love, and so it would be like having her hand in his whenever he walked about town.

'I have something for you, too,' he revealed with shy modesty, stealing into his pocket and proffering her a present wrapped with silver paper and gold thread. His wife attempted to compose herself, but curiosity got the better of her, so she snatched it from him with impatient impishness, and turning it over and over in her hands, Margaret's senses explored it keenly. At last, when she opened it, out fell another pair of somethings, but these were very different indeed. In her hands, she held two turtle doves, handsomely carved from white marble and porcelain.

'John!' she breathed, her heart all in a flutter. 'Where did you —'

'I made them,' he confessed nervously. 'I have watched you, Meg, sewing and knitting all your lovely things, and it occurred to me that you are always giving to others, so I wanted to give you something, but not something that was bought, rather, something that was manufactured with my own two tradesman's hands,' he said, holding them up to her so that she could see the scars that scored his skin from years of industry.

'I cannot knit you gloves or a scarf,' he acknowledged, disregarding the fact that he had already tried and failed. 'But I am good with tools, so I shaped these. They are formed mainly from stone, but also in part from the teacup you served me on the first night I came to take tea here, the same one you gave me last Christmas Eve. I know them to be one and the same, because the cup had a small crack under the handle, so I took it and made these. I thought about it for weeks. I kept starting on something and then tossing it away, nothing felt right. But then I thought of all that you mean to me, and all that Christmas means to me now that it represents the beginning of our shared love, so what better symbol to give you than these? They are an emblem of hope and faith and the loyal commitment they make to each other. They are…two friends,' he enlightened, praying that she did not think him too ridiculous.

Margaret, who had been studying her gift, raised her head to look at her husband, her eyes welling with tears. She was quick to throw her arms around him and pressed her lips to the spot just below his cravat where she could see a patch of skin peeking out.

John enveloped his arms around her and drew his wife near. '*Take care*,' he whispered into her ear, reciting words of old. '*If you do not speak – I shall claim you as my own in some strange presumptuous way.*'

Margaret snuffled, nestling her face in the crook of his neck. 'I love you, John Thornton,' she proclaimed, weeping with tears of unadulterated happiness.

'I love you, Margaret Thornton,' he said in turn, rubbing his nose against hers.

Staring into her eyes, and never once looking away, John reached into his pocket and pulled out a single stem of mistletoe. His wife blushed coyly to understand his meaning, recalling the previous

Christmas Eve when they had shared the first delicious meeting of their mouths on the street outside, the snow-blossoms falling all around them in fluffy clusters of crisp white. Grinning mischievously, John held it high above their heads and leaned in closer, as did Margaret, and their lips merged as one, locked and lost in a lover's kiss.

After a while, Margaret stood to gently arrange the doves on the tree, the two of them promising to watch over this happy home. It was then that she was distracted by a light outside, and going to the window, she watched as a mass of clouds scattered in the sky, giving way to a constellation of twinkling stars that shone big and bright, casting their triumphant glow across Milton, celebrating the day that Christ was born.

Sighing contentedly, Margaret hummed as she felt her husband come behind her, wrapping both her and their son in his secure embrace. Margaret was about to reach out to pull the curtain closed, but was soon halted when John cried out: '*No!*,' and she stilled her hand at once.

Realising that his tone had been sharp, John nuzzled the back of her neck in apology and amiably requested that she leave it be. Nevertheless, Margaret continued to show her confusion with a cock of her head and the cockle of her brow.

'You never know who may be looking,' John defended with an air of mystery. 'You never know who may need to witness a scene like this. Perhaps there is a lost and lonely soul out there who needs to hope tonight, and who are we to deny them it?'

His wife still did not entirely understand him, but the earnestness in his voice told her all she needed to know, so tilting back, Margaret melted into her husband's arms. They stood like this for what felt like hours, simply content to be together again, a family of three.

As the clock chimed the hour, heralding the dawning of a new Christmas Day, the couple wondered if there was anyone out there in the wide and wonderful world, who, in years to come, would care for them and their humble little story. Hence, if someone should so happen to seek to find them here, preserved in these timeless pages, penned with the permanent ink of everlasting love, then they whisper upon the northern wind these words of eternal friendship to you:

'We wish you a merry Christmas,
and a happy New Year!'

The End

Quotes

This book has chosen to include a selection of quotes from Gaskell's novel. The purpose of this is not an attempt to copy her in any way, but rather, to celebrate her genius by interweaving her narrative and dialogue amongst my own, more humble scribbles. In addition, it helps us to appreciate the value of her brilliance, of how the sentiments of her writing can be so seamlessly transported from one literary work to another, showing us that it can transcend the barriers of time and text. And lastly, I am aware that some readers may never have read *North and South*, and so I hope and trust that this may encourage them to do so, for it is a most wonderful book indeed.

Every effort has been made to emphasise any incorporated quotes in italics throughout *The Woollen Olive Branch*, thus highlighting that they are not my own work, but that of Gaskell's. However, there may be occasions when the font embedding does not effectively translate from the manuscript to the final product, so please see below the quotes that have been included for further reference.

Chapter 2:
But the future must be met, however stern and iron it be.

Chapter 3:
Margaret liked this smile; it was the first thing she had admired in this new friend of her father's; and the

opposition of character, shown in all these details of appearance she had just been noticing, seemed to explain the attraction they evidently felt towards each other.

'I dare say there's many a woman makes as sad a mistake as I have done, and only finds it out too late.'

Chapter 4:
'Is Miss Hale so remarkable for truth?'

Chapter 5:
...he could have bitten his tongue out. What was he? And why should he stab her with her shame in that way? How evil he had been that night; possessed by ill-humour at being detained so long from her; irritated by the mention of some name, because he thought it belonged to a more successful lover; ill-tempered because he had been unable to cope, with a light heart, against one who was trying, by gay and careless speeches, to make the evening pass pleasantly away, — the kind old friend to all parties, whose manner by this time might be well known to Mr Thornton, who had been acquainted with him for many years.

She had not risen to leave the room, as she had done in former days, when his abruptness or his temper had annoyed her. She sat quite still, after the first momentary glance of grieved surprise, that made her eyes look like some child's who has met with an unexpected rebuff; they slowly dilated into mournful, reproachful sadness; and then they fell, and she bent over her work, and did not speak again. But he could not help looking at her, and he saw a sigh tremble over her body, as if she quivered in some unwonted chill. He gave short sharp answers; he was uneasy and cross, unable to discern between jest and earnest; anxious only for a look, a word of hers, before which to prostrate himself in penitent humility. But she neither looked nor spoke. Her round taper fingers flew in and out of her sewing, as steadily and swiftly as if that were the business of her life. She could not care for him, he thought, or else the passionate fervour of his wish would have forced her to raise those eyes, if but for an instant, to read the late repentance in his. He could have struck her before he left, in order that by some strange overt act of rudeness, he might earn the privilege of telling her the remorse that gnawed at his heart. It was well that the long walk in the open air wound up that evening for him. It sobered him back into grave resolution, that henceforth he would see as little of her as possible, — since the very sight of that face arid form, the very sounds of that voice (like the soft winds of pure melody) had such power to move him from his balance.

Well! He had known what love was – a sharp pang, a fierce experience, in the midst of whose flames he was struggling! but, through that furnace he would fight his way out into the serenity of middle age, - all the richer and more human for having known this great passion.

Chapter 8:
Those who are happy and successful themselves are too apt to make light of the misfortunes of others.

Chapter 9:
For all his pain, he longed to see the author of it. Although he hated Margaret at times, when he thought of that gentle familiar attitude and all the attendant circumstances, he had a restless desire to renew her picture in his mind - a longing for the very atmosphere she breathed. He was in the Charybdis of passion, and must perforce circle and circle ever nearer round the fatal centre.

Chapter 10:
He knew how she would love. He had not loved her without gaining that instinctive knowledge of what capabilities were in her. Her soul would walk in glorious sunlight if any man was worthy, by his power of loving, to win back her love.

Chapter 13:
She was so tired - so tired of being whirled on through all these phases of life, in which nothing abides, no creature, no place; it is like the circle in which the victims of earthly passion eddy continually.

Come poor little heart! be cheery and brave. We'll be a great deal to one another, if we are thrown off and left desolate.

Chapter 14:

'Take care. If you do not speak – I shall claim you as my own in some strange presumptuous way.'

Glossary of Terms

This story has included a series of Victorian and Mancunian terms so that it might seek to link the past and the present through the use of authentic words and dialect. Details of the phrases and their meanings can be found below.

Chapter 4: Mafficking: When people took to the streets and exhibited rowdy behaviour.

Chapter 4: Gal-sneaker: A man who was devoted to seduction.

Chapter 5: Pigeon-livered: Being a coward or cowardly.

Chapter 7: Bit o' Raspberries: An attractive girl, originally a raspberry jam as this was considered the most flavoursome of preserves, so the prettiest of the girls were a bit o' raspberry. However, this also came to mean someone who was overly sweet and ripe.

Chapter 7: Foozler: Someone who tended to be clumsy or awkward.

Chapter 12: Ginnels: Mancunian (Manchester), term for alleyways.

Chapter 12: Clinkerbells: Hampshire dialect term for icicles.

Chapter 12: Hibernacle: A place to retreat from the world in wintertime.

Chapter 12: Mufflements: Lancashire dialect term for warm and insulating clothing.

Chapter 12: Mithering: Fussing over someone.

Chapter 13: Dizzying Age: Getting elderly.

Chapter 13: Church-bell: A talkative woman.

Chapter 13: Gigglemug: A perpetually smiling face.

Acknowledgements

I would like to thank Sandy Welch for granting permission for this book to be written, since it contains references to her exceptional screenplay. I would also like to thank her for the wonderful opportunity to meet her in 2022, so that I could interview her about her time working on *North and South* whilst also supporting Elizabeth Gaskell's House. It was a privilege and a pleasure, so from one writer to another, thank you.

I cannot go without thanking my husband, Scott, for all his love and support over the years in encouraging my writing and helping me whenever and however he could. I want to especially thank him for all his patience with me as I finished and formatted this story over Christmas 2022. I could not have done it without you, Powges, watching our little Bee while I scribbled.

I want to thank Elaine Owen for all her comradely support over the past year. Elaine is an exceptional writer and a "brilliant" person. Not only has her impressive creative efforts and energy encouraged my own, but she has been a fount of advice on publishing and the world of fan fiction, and for that, I will be eternally grateful.

And lastly, and most importantly, I would also like to thank all the lovely ladies who have been such dedicated readers over the past couple of years, women who have shown me unfailing support, helping me to shape my work, get on with it when I'm feeling tired or low, and reminded me that my scribbles do matter. Here's to you: Rhona, Denise, Helena, Deirdre, Catherine, Anna, Michelle, Dawn, Halin, Julia, Stacye and Katlyn, and those of you who have quietly yet faithfully followed my journey so far. I hope you will stick around for more, because there is much more to come. (Also, all your names end in an a, e or n, what's up with that, guys?)

Declaration

While *The Woollen Olive Branch* has been written entirely by myself, I must give Elizabeth Gaskell full credit and applause for writing the original novel on which it is based. Again, while the majority of the story contains my own words, there are a few quotes from the primary text penned by Gaskell, all presented in italics for the purpose of giving recognition to the author, and highlighting them for the benefit of readers. Furthermore, while *North and South* is now in the public domain, and no longer under copyright restrictions, potentially interested parties relating to Gaskell have been advised of its publication for the sake of maintaining positive working relationships.

This book has taken the liberty of referring to the fictional character of Ann Latimer, a person who does not exist in the original novel, but is a creation of Sandy Welch's for the 2004 BBC screen adaptation of *North and South*. I would like to note that while Sandy Welch and the BBC have granted permission for this book to be published, they have no further association with this work.

This book has no commercial connection with any societies or trusts relating to any persons or organisations that may have been involved in the writing and creating of the novel or the series, and any promotion or support shown by them following its publication will be by their own choice and discretion.

About the Author

Hello, my name is Caroline Malcolm-Boulton, also known as The Scribbler CMB. Born in 1993, I'm a British writer who lives in Scotland with my husband and our daughter.

I first came across *North and South* at age eleven when the 2004 BBC series aired. Growing up in a family that had always cherished the classics, we were excited every time a new adaptation came to our screens, so it was a real treat to sit down and watch it together. Even so, I'm sorry to say, that like most people, we'd never heard of *North and South* before, given that Elizabeth Gaskell did not, and still does not, get the recognition she deserves. Still, while her lack of appreciation is inequitable, it did have a silver lining, which was that we were able to watch it without knowing what was to come.

And well, it goes without saying that I fell in love immediately.

Over the last eighteen years, my fascination with *North and South* has continued to grow. I read and watch it frequently; I studied it at university; and I was involved in a touring stage adaptation of it in 2015, helping to write the script and also being privileged to play Fanny Thornton. Now, on the brink of my thirties, I work part-time as a freelance Arts and Film&Television journalist, and am delighted to say that I've dedicated much of my time to exploring the life and legacy of Gaskell, most recently supporting

Elizabeth Gaskell's House with some of their marvellous events.

But what about writing *North and South* retellings and continuations? Well, despite admiring and appreciating the Victorian classic for almost two decades, it wasn't until 2020 that I discovered fan fiction. I'd heard of it before, but to be honest, I didn't really understand it, and I thought it was a bit odd. However, when Covid-19 hit, for various reasons that I won't bore you with, I thought about trying fanfic to pass the time.

It proved to be one of the best decisions of my life.

I quickly became aware of the diversity out there in terms of styles, takes on characters and themes, and even quality of writing. Some stories were exceptional, doing Gaskell justice, and some were not to my taste at all. It's remarkable to see the infinite number of options there are for new storylines, and each writer clearly has a very personal relationship with *North and South,* again emphasising its value, demonstrating how it overcomes the barriers of time and culture. But then I realised something. If these people had the right to write their respective interpretations of my favourite book, then why couldn't I?

So I did.

It's been an incredible journey, one which I hope is far from over, and I've learnt a lot about myself, grown as a writer and reader, and met some wonderful fellow fans along the way. It's also prompted me to encourage others to write, because I strongly feel that writing has numerous benefits in terms of a person's cognitive and creative welfare, and I've been proud as punch to see so many friends take up the pen. Fan fiction is a unique genre, and I appreciate if some feel unsure about it, but I'd highly recommend giving it a go. I always say that reading a new book, an original book, is like going on an adventure, we don't know where it's going to take us. But reading fan fiction is like coming home to something familiar and safe, to people and places that we hold dear in our hearts, and there are no two characters I hold more dear than John and Margaret.

So there you have it, I'm just a woman who loves to read and write, and actually, that was all I needed to say.

Contact:
Email: caroline.malcolmboultonmedia@gmail.com
Twitter: @TheScribblerCMB
Facebook Arts Page: @TheScribblerCMBArts
Facebook Writing Page: @TheScribblerCMBWriter
Instagram: @TheScribblerCMB

Printed in Great Britain
by Amazon

32692097R00126